SHOTS
FIRED

Visit us at www.boldstrokesbooks.com

What Reviewers Say About Bold Strokes Books

"With its expected unexpected twists, vivid characters and healthy dose of humor, *Blind Curves* is a very fun read that will keep you guessing." – *Bay Windows*

"In a succinct film style narrative, with scenes that move, a character-driven plot, and crisp dialogue worthy of a screenplay ... the Richfield and Rivers novels are ... an engaging Hollywood mystery ... series." – *Midwest Book Review*

Force of Nature "...is filled with nonstop, fast paced action. Tornadoes, raging fire blazes, heroic and daring rescues... Baldwin does a fine job of describing the fast-paced scenes and inspiring the reader to keep on turning the pages." – *L-word.comLiterature*

In the Jude Devine mystery series the "...characters seem fully capable of walking away from the particulars of whodunit and engaging the reader in other aspects of their lives." – *Lambda Book Report*

Mine "...weaves a tale of yearning, love, lust, and conflict resolution ... a believable plot, with strong characters in a charming setting." – *JustAboutWrite*

"While these two women struggle with their issues, there is some very, very hot sex. If you enjoy complex characters and passionate sex scenes, you'll love *Wild Abandon*." – *MegaScene*

"*Course of Action* is a romance ... populated with a host of captivating and amiable characters. The glimpses into the lifestyles of the rich and beautiful people are rather like guilty pleasures ... a most satisfying and entertaining reading experience." – *Midwest Book Review*

The Clinic is "...a spellbinding novel." – *JustAboutWrite*

"*Unexpected Sparks* lived up to its promise and was thoroughly enjoyable ... Dartt did a lovely job at building the relationship between Kate and Nikki." – *Lambda Book Report*

"*Sequestered Hearts* ... is everything a romance should be. It is teeming with longing, heartbreak, and of course, love. As pure romances go, it is one of the best in print today." – *L-word.comLiterature*

"*The Exile and the Sorcerer* is a mesmerizing read, a tour-de-force packed with adventure, ordeals, complex twists and turns, and the internal introspection of appealing characters." – *Midwest Book Review*

The Spanish Pearl is "...both science fiction and romance in this adventurous tale ... A most entertaining read, with a sequel already in the works. Hot, hot, hot!" – *Minnesota Literature*

"A deliciously sexy thriller ... *Dark Valentine* is funny, scary, and very realistic. The story is tightly written and keeps the reader gripped to the exciting end." – *JustAbout Write*

"*Punk Like Me* ... is different. It is engaging. It is life-affirming. Frankly, it is genius. This is a rare book in that it has a soul; one that is laid bare for all to see." – *JustAboutWrite*

"*Chance* is not a novel about the music industry; it is about a woman discovering herself as she muddles through all the trappings of fame." – *Midwest Book Review*

Sweet Creek "... is sublimely in tune with the times." – *Q-Syndicate*

"*Forever Found* ... neatly combines hot sex scenes, humor, engaging characters, and an exciting story." – *MegaScene*

Shield of Justice is a "...well-plotted...lovely romance...I couldn't turn the pages fast enough!" – Ann Bannon, author of *The Beebo Brinker Chronicles*

The 100th Generation is "...filled with ancient myths, Egyptian gods and goddesses, legends, and, most wonderfully, it contains the lesbian equivalent of Indiana Jones living and working in modern Egypt." – *Just About Write*

Sword of the Guardian is "...a terrific adventure, coming of age story, a romance, and tale of courtly intrigue, attempted assassination, and gender confusion ... a rollicking fun book and a must-read for those who enjoy courtly light fantasy in a medieval-seeming time." – *Midwest Book Review*

"*Of Drag Kings and the Wheel of Fate*'s lush rush of a romance incorporates reincarnation, a grounded transman and his peppy daughter, and the dark moods of a troubled witch—wonderful homage to Leslie Feinberg's classic gender-bending novel, *Stone Butch Blues*." – *Q-Syndicate*

In *Running with the Wind* "...the discussions of the nature of sex, love, power, and sexuality are insightful and represent a welcome voice from the view of late-20-something characters today." – *Midwest Book Review*

"Rich in character portrayal, *The Devil Inside* is an unusual, unpredictable, and thought-provoking love story that will have the reader questioning the definition of right and wrong long after she finishes the book." – *JustAboutWrite*

Wall of Silence "...is perfectly plotted and has a very real voice and consistently accurate tone, which is not always the case with lesbian mysteries." – *Midwest Book Review*

SHOTS FIRED

by

MJ Williamz

2008

SHOTS FIRED

ISBN 10: 1-60282-035-X
ISBN 13: 978-1-60282-035-7

THIS TRADE PAPERBACK ORIGINAL IS PUBLISHED BY
BOLD STROKES BOOKS, INC.
P.O. BOX 249
VALLEY FALLS, NY 12185

FIRST EDITION: NOVEMBER 2008

CREDITS
EDITOR: JENNIFER KNIGHT AND STACIA SEAMAN
PRODUCTION DESIGN: STACIA SEAMAN
COVER DESIGN BY SHERI (GRAPHICARTIST2020@HOTMAIL.COM)

Acknowledgments

This is my first book, and therefore, there are so many people to thank.

There's my partner, who's been introducing me as an author for a lot longer than I've considered myself one. And our son Caleb, who, through his own writing, challenged me to raise the level of mine.

Thank you to all of you who have been on this wild ride with me. I hope you know who you are. You believed in me when I didn't believe in myself. And you never let me quit. I owe you so much.

Last, but not least, thank you, Rad, for this awesome opportunity, and Jennifer, for sharing that joyous experience called editing. Without you two, none of this would be happening.

Thank you. Thank you. Thank you.

Dedication

For T and CJ—for everything.

CHAPTER ONE

L ady, listen to me. We called 911. Help is on the way."

Lost in a fog, teetering on the brink of consciousness, Kyla Edmonds recognized the feel of the steering wheel under her head. Her chest rested on an unknown object that was hard and uncomfortable. She tried to make sense of the chaos around her. Voices were audible in the distance. She sensed people milling around, just out of sight. She tried to push herself up to a sitting position and winced. Pain shot through her head, sides, and left leg. Her head bumped into something hard and she let it fall back onto the steering wheel.

A man's face appeared in the window. "Can you hear me, lady?"

The window? She was in her car. But where?

Kyla's head hurt. The inside throbbed, while the outside felt like someone had stuck needles into her scalp. The slightest movement made the pain more severe, so she tried to hold her head still and survey the scene by moving her eyes only. The area seemed to be lit by a spotlight, but she couldn't tell where she was. Somehow that was important to her. A giant tree loomed a few feet from her face. The bark was rough and chunky, like a pine. She thought she should know where a giant pine stood, but she couldn't remember. If she could just place it, she knew she'd feel better, more in control.

"Hang on, lady. They're almost here." The voice sounded even farther away and the face in the window was fuzzy.

Kyla felt herself drifting. Desperately trying to make sense of what was happening, she forced herself to replay the events of the day, hoping to determine how she ended up here.

It had been busy at the office. January was always busy for accountants. She remembered leaving late. Or was that the day before? Something important lurked just outside her memory's edge. She closed her eyes, weak and frustrated.

"Stay with us, lady. Come on. Open your eyes."

She wanted to sleep, but she made herself stay awake by tuning in to a conversation going on outside the car.

"That's a lot of blood. Where the hell is the ambulance?"

"Look at the roof. It's caved in. She's lucky she's alive."

"Did you guys hear shots?"

Kyla forced her eyes open and tried to focus on the men talking. Shots? What did they mean? And whose blood? She felt a warm stickiness running down her cheek. Were they talking about *her* blood? She wanted to ask them, but she couldn't summon the energy.

Her mind floated back to leaving the office. Why did it matter so much that she had been running late? As a CPA, she could work five hours one day and twelve the next. She remembered that it had been important for her to leave on time today, but why?

She heard someone mention the shots again and a man said, "Yeah, like gunshots."

Why were they talking about gunshots? Why didn't any of these people help her instead of standing around talking?

What day was it? Friday? Yes, Friday. *Friday*. Colton had

guitar lessons. Oh, no. She panicked. Where was Colton? Was he in the car? She tried to turn her head, desperate to see if her fifteen-year-old son was in the passenger seat, but the pain was too much. She groaned with the effort.

"Oh, God." This time a woman's voice. "Listen to her. Isn't there anything we can do?"

"No way," a man responded. "We could hurt her more if we try. The paramedics will get here soon."

"Gunshots?" The other conversation continued. "Here? I heard something. I thought it was kids shooting off some fireworks left over from New Year's Eve."

"Maybe."

Who cares about fireworks? Kyla wanted to scream. *Just get me out of here.*

She heard sirens. If she could just hold on, she could ask what happened. The voices faded, replaced by the high-pitched wail. When the siren died, she could make out the flurry of activity. The roar of an idling engine, doors slamming, people yelling to each other, and the sound of movement around the car.

"Ma'am, can you hear me?" Someone banged on the window.

Kyla was cold, so very cold. Why weren't they hurrying to get her out?

"Is she away from the door?" a man asked.

"You've got room," came the response.

Suddenly the night air was filled with a horrible screech. Kyla felt as if her head would explode. Just to the left of her, a pair of giant metal pliers cut through the car body and started to peel the roof back. Kyla's head bounced off the wheel and crashed back as the car lurched. Cold flowed over her from top to bottom. Again she tried to see if Colton was with her.

The pain was still too much to bear. She wanted to be in her own bed with Echo by her side. She prayed that this was just a nightmare.

Suddenly there were hands on her, easing her to an upright position. Something soft yet unyielding closed around her neck and a man said, "This is a cervical collar, ma'am. It will keep your neck from moving. We don't want to take any chances."

"Backboard's ready," she heard. "Ease her seat back."

She felt herself slowly reclining until she was almost horizontal.

"Unhook her seat belt. Lady, stay with us."

With great effort she opened her eyes. Seat belt? That must have been what was cutting into her chest. She moved her gaze constantly, trying to follow the voices, determined to ask where she was, but her voice wouldn't come.

She heard, "One. Two. Three," and her rescuers slid her from her seat and onto a hard, flat surface.

"Strap her down and let's get her out of here."

As they carried her away from the wreckage, she looked around. The area was rural and seemed familiar, but the undeveloped grassland could have been anywhere. The solitary pine tree meant something, she was sure. But its significance was lost as she finally closed her eyes and gave herself over to the blackness.

❖

"A gunshot wound to the head." Detective Pat Silverton skimmed the report the hospital had faxed to the Bidwell Police Department. "And they didn't say if it happened before or after the accident." She returned the report to her partner, Detective Tom Magnell.

The hulking bald man leafed impatiently through the pages again. "Nah. Just that she's got a gunshot wound, plus cuts all over her head, four broken ribs, and a broken left leg. You gotta assume the lacerations and broken bones were from the accident."

Pat supposed that assumption was reasonable, although it was possible that Kyla Edmonds had been beaten up before she got in the car. She didn't put forward that idea. Even at five feet eight, she felt small compared to her partner, but her stature had nothing to do with a sense that she was somehow inadequate. Lack of experience made her feel that way.

"I guess it happened near her home," she said. "Lone Pine is just up Monroe Drive from her neighborhood, and they still haven't broken ground on that new development yet. It's one of the few open areas left off Monroe."

"Any ideas?"

"I'd say we're looking for someone she knows." The possibility seemed even more likely if Edmonds had sustained some of her injuries before the crash. Pat made a vague observation. "I guess the doctors would have known if she was hurt before she ever got into the car."

Magnell's blue eyes narrowed a little. Predictably, he claimed the theory as his own. "I was just thinking that. There could be some kind of staged situation going on here. She takes a beating. The attacker puts her in the driver seat and sends the car toward the tree. When she isn't killed, he tries to finish her off with one to the head."

Pat thought the angle for that shot would be next to impossible once the crash had already happened, but she decided that was the kind of theory they could examine later. She would leave it to an expert to reconstruct the crime and calculate the timing of the gunshot. For now, she was content that she'd given Magnell something to think about.

He motioned to the hospital room behind them. "You ready to get a statement?" Barely waiting for Pat's nod, he said, "Let's do it."

She knocked politely before opening the door and entering the room. A small, pale figure lay motionless beneath the bedcovers. One of her limp hands was held by a woman sitting in the chair next to the bed. She released the hand and stood. She was tall and wore green sweatpants and a gray hooded sweatshirt with *Oregon* printed across the chest. Her face was drawn and her short dark hair stuck out in all directions, looking like it hadn't been brushed in days. She seemed immediately on edge, almost distrustful.

Magnell identified himself and offered his hand, which was taken hesitantly. Indicating Pat, he said, "This is my partner Detective Silverton. And you are?"

"Echo Flannery." A pair of ice-cold blue eyes skipped past Magnell to Pat, anger in their depths. "This is not a good time."

"We need to talk to the victim," Magnell said.

"The victim?" Echo seemed incredulous.

"Yeah." Magnell scanned the paperwork. "A Miss Edmonds."

"This is Ms. Kyla Edmonds." Echo gestured toward the unconscious woman. "As you can see, she isn't in any shape to talk to you."

"And what relation are you to her?"

"I'm her partner."

Magnell exchanged a look with Pat. She could almost hear his mental cogs turning. Lesbians, and maybe one had beat up on the other, then tried to shoot her. His eyes took on the attack-dog glint Pat had come to know after two years working with him as a detective for Bidwell PD.

He reached for Kyla's shoulder, but Echo grabbed his arm. "I said no."

Yanking his arm from her grasp, he towered over her and asked, "Is there some reason you don't want us talking to her?"

"Yes, a very good reason. She's unconscious."

"And I bet you'd be happy if she stayed that way, wouldn't you?"

"What the hell is that supposed to mean?" Echo leaned into Magnell, seemingly trying to get in his face.

Hastily, Pat asked, "Has she woken up at all since last night, Ms. Flannery?"

Her attempt to defuse the tension was not well received. Pat groaned inwardly. Her partner was not known for his bedside manner and really didn't like to be told no. The fact that he was from the good ol' boy network made hearing "no" much worse when it came from a woman.

Echo and Magnell shared a strained silence, each eyeballing the other like someone might take a swing. Pat could tell that if she didn't get him out of the room soon, he was going to provoke Flannery even more. He believed in shaking up interview subjects to see how they would react. His theory was that a percentage of people with guilty consciences would spill their guts the moment a detective showed suspicion. He thought it was worth aggravating innocent parties to nail that percentage.

Echo's gaze finally shifted to Pat. "She hasn't stayed conscious for any length of time. She seems to surface sometimes, and she moves a bit, but then she's gone again. I keep talking to her, but she doesn't answer."

"Since she can't give us any information now, we'll come back tomorrow," Pat said.

"If she's still alive then." Magnell sneered.

"What the fuck?" Echo's face was flushed with anger. "She's in serious condition, not critical. It's just a matter of time before she comes to."

"How do you feel about that likelihood?" Magnell's tone was filled with suspicion.

"What are you implying?"

"Where were you last night between five and eight?"

Echo put her hands on her hips. "You're kidding, right?"

"Do I look like I'm kidding?" Magnell's eyes were mere slits. "Just answer the question. Friday night, say six o'clock-ish?"

"I was at work."

Magnell looked dubious. "That's kind of late, isn't it?"

"Not for me."

"So I'm guessing you have people who can vouch for you?"

"Only if you count the thirty or so employees and customers."

"What do you do, Ms. Flannery?" Pat asked.

"I own Echo's Cardio. It's a gym in Bidwell."

Pat nodded. She had never been inside the place, but she could recall driving past it. It was in a renovated warehouse in old town. "What time did you leave on Friday?"

"As soon as the hospital called me."

"Can anyone confirm that?" Pat asked politely.

Echo sighed, clearly exasperated. "My assistant, Meadow Tenori. She was in my office when I took the call."

Magnell scribbled in his notebook. "We're gonna check out your story, so now's the time to tell us if you've left out anything we should know."

Echo cocked her head. In a sarcastic tone she replied,

"Actually, if you must know, I was out taking target practice."

"Laugh now," Magnell said. "We'll see how funny you really are soon."

"Sometime over the next few days, it would be helpful if we could interview you at the station," Pat said quickly. "We don't need to take a full statement here."

"Thank you." Echo's hands fell from her hips and she stared down at the woman in the bed. "Now seriously, please leave. She can't tell you anything."

Magnell glared at her for a moment before reminding her dourly, "We'll be back tomorrow."

"I can't wait," Echo muttered as the door closed behind them.

CHAPTER TWO

S he's hiding something." Magnell couldn't wait till they made it to the car. "We need to see if her alibi pans out ASAP."

Pat kept her thoughts to herself as they crossed the parking lot to their unmarked Lincoln.

"What? You don't agree?" Magnell asked as they climbed into the car.

"I don't disagree about checking her alibi. I'm just not convinced she's hiding something."

"Come on. You saw her. She was immediately defensive when she saw us. And she did everything in her power to keep us from talking to the vic."

"The victim was unconscious," Pat reminded him.

"You know where this gym is? Where are we going?" Magnell asked, starting the car.

"It's in Old Town. So let's say Flannery has something to do with the shooting and the accident. Why is she hanging around the hospital? Why doesn't she make a break for it? She could be long gone by now."

"That's easy. She's playing the part of caring, concerned... *friend*. She figures she can make a good impression no one will look at her as a suspect. I'm telling you, that whole scene was an act."

"Or she could genuinely be a caring and concerned partner who felt we were there to harass Edmonds. She's frustrated, worried, and scared and didn't want us to do anything to further harm her partner."

"Well, the only way we're gonna prove this one way or the other is to thoroughly investigate her. Maybe she had a reason for wanting Edmonds dead. Maybe she's at the hospital because she's looking for a way to finish the job."

"Okay. Let's say you're right. Let's say she wants her gone. Why? Money? Does Edmonds have money? Maybe an insurance policy? Why would Flannery need that? She owns her own business, for God's sake."

"What if business isn't booming? If she's about to lose it? I'm guessing her ego wouldn't take that too well, and a healthy insurance check would certainly solve that problem Then again, maybe there's someone else? Another woman? God only knows with their type. She may be bored with this Edmonds woman and ready to move on."

"We need to find out how long they've been together, for starters. And anyway, if she's met someone else, why not just leave Edmonds? Why try to kill her?"

"Maybe she told her she wanted out and Edmonds refused to let her go."

"We're almost there." Pat pointed. "It's that single-story brick building on the left up there."

As he parked the car, Magnell laid out the game plan. "We'll find this Meadow Tenori and see what light she can shed on Flannery. If she's her right-hand woman, she would know if the business is going bust."

"And if she's loyal, she might not share anything she thinks might be incriminating."

"Or maybe she wants to cooperate with the police and will talk openly about business problems and any girlfriends Flannery has on the side."

They got out of the car and walked toward Echo's Cardio, just one of the many renovated buildings down by the railroad tracks in Old Bidwell.

Magnell let out a low whistle as they entered the club. "Get a load of this equipment. We're talkin' top of the line."

Pat gazed longingly at the state-of-the-art machines lined up in the large, open room. She wondered what the cost of a membership was. She was sure she'd never be able to afford it on a cop's salary. "Let's just get this over with." She nudged her partner toward a tight blonde at the front desk.

Magnell waved his badge and said, "Where can we find Meadow Tenori?"

The blonde directed them to an office on the far side of the gym. Pat was thankful that the gym was almost empty so she didn't have to suffer through Magnell drooling over a room full of scantily-clad women working out.

The office door opened and a petite redhead with short, spiky hair invited them in. Magnell didn't bother to hide his lusting stare as they identified themselves and followed the woman to the desk across the room. Pat had a feeling her appreciation for the expanse of thigh below the micro-skirt was just as obvious.

The hottie motioned to two chairs across from her. "What can I do for you, Detectives?"

Magnell took this for his cue to radiate the power of his position. Stretching his legs in front of him, he settled back in his chair with one hand resting on his holster. "Miss Tenori—"

"Just Meadow. No Miss or Ms. or whatever."

"Fine, Meadow," Magnell continued. "Can you tell us what your title is here?"

"I'm the assistant director. Look, is there a problem? Because if we're in trouble or something, I really need to call my boss."

"No. You're not in trouble. No reason to call your boss. That would be Ms. Flannery, right?"

"Yes." Meadow sat straighter and crossed her arms over her chest.

Pat sensed that she was already on the defensive. That didn't bode well for the interview. She wondered if Echo Flannery had already phoned to let her assistant know what was happening, and perhaps to build her own alibi, if she had something to hide. "Meadow, we're here to ask some routine questions in relation to an incident on Friday night. Are you aware of what happened to Ms. Flannery's partner?"

"I heard she crashed her car. Is she okay?"

"Hopefully," Pat replied. "So, you've spoken with Ms. Flannery since the accident?"

"Sure. She called me on her cell right away. From the hospital."

"What did she say?" Magnell asked.

Meadow looked slightly bewildered. "She told me she wouldn't be coming in to work since she needs to be with Kyla. Look, if there's something you want to know, you probably need to talk to her."

"We did." Somehow Magnell managed to make that sound ominous.

Meadow frowned. "I don't understand. Why do you need to talk to me, then?"

Magnell ignored the question. "When did Ms. Flannery leave on Friday evening?"

"I'm not sure what the time was. She went as soon as the hospital called. It was terrible. She said Kyla had been in a car accident and—"

"Was she here all evening up until that point?" Magnell asked.

"Yes. Friday's one of our busiest nights. She's always here."

"You saw her yourself?"

"Everyone did." Meadow shifted in her chair. Unease seeped into her expression. "Why are you asking these questions? Is something wrong?"

Pat smiled reassuringly. "It's all routine, Meadow. We just need some background information. Let's start simple. How long have you worked here?"

"Six years."

"And how long have you been Ms. Flannery's right-hand woman?"

"Four years."

"How's business?" Magnell waved a hand in the direction of the gym. "Must cost a bundle to run this place."

"It does, but Echo's built the club up a lot over the years. We're in pretty good shape."

"Looks like it." Magnell's eyes dropped to her breasts.

"What kind of boss is Ms. Flannery?" Pat asked.

"She's a great boss. All her employees love her." She blushed.

Pat pretended not to notice the sideways glance Magnell cast her way. "All of them? Are you saying no one has ever left on bad terms? There's never been a…problem situation with a staff member?" Pat chuckled softly. "Sounds like an incredible work environment."

"Yeah." Magnell twirled his ballpoint in obvious disbelief. True to form, he added, "Not exactly what we've heard."

The ploy was one all detectives used to pump information. If they pretended prior knowledge, background witnesses didn't agonize about revealing secrets.

Meadow's face reddened further. "I'm not saying it's perfect." She hesitated. "We did have a…situation recently."

"Let's hear your version of those events." Magnell's tone was resigned, as though they knew the story well but would tolerate hearing it again.

"I don't know what you've heard, but I don't think you can believe everything people say."

Interested that she was already defending her boss, Pat said, "That's how we feel, too. And that's why we talk to people like you, who are in a position to know the truth."

Meadow sighed. "Well, like everyone else, I heard the rumors that Echo was messing around with a woman who worked here. Jenny Vasquez."

Magnell leaned forward and rested his elbows on his beefy thighs. "They were having an affair?"

"Look. I think Kyla's great, so I don't want to see her hurt."

"She's already hurt," Pat said carefully. "And our job is to find out what happened to her and why. All you're doing is answering questions to help us get to the bottom of this."

Meadow looked pained. "Well, I didn't believe it at first, but Echo was here a lot when Jenny started. I mean, she was *always* here. And Jenny was always in Echo's office. With the door closed."

"Does Ms. Flannery usually keep the door open?"

"Yes."

"What are you getting at?" Magnell was obviously enjoying this thread. "You think they were carrying on right here?"

"I don't honestly know. They weren't obvious around us. You know, flirting and teasing and stuff."

"They were trying to keep it discreet?" Pat asked.

"I think so. After a while, Echo wasn't around as much and Jenny would show up late for work or leave early. Or skip out for a long break in the middle of the day. We all figured she was sneaking out to see Echo, so they didn't have to worry about leaving together and having us all talk."

"Is Jenny still employed here?" Pat could almost smell Magnell's hands sweating with anticipation. At this rate they would have a motive and a suspect by the end of the day.

"No, Echo had me fire her about a month ago."

Magnell's ballpoint was suddenly still. "Why?"

"Jenny was telling everyone about the affair. It pissed Echo off and she told me to fire her."

"Do you usually do the hiring and firing?" Pat asked.

"It depends. I mean, it's not unusual for me to fire someone."

"Did Echo ever talk to you about the affair?"

"She said nothing happened and Jenny was trying to cause problems."

"But you're not convinced."

"I can't imagine anybody with a pulse turning Jenny Vasquez down."

"A real looker?"

"Sure. Dark skin, sexy eyes, long silky hair, and tits for days." Meadow grinned. "What can I say?"

Pat had to laugh, but her partner didn't seem as amused.

"How long did Vasquez work here?" he asked.

Meadow chewed on the inside of her cheek and stared at the ceiling before answering. "Maybe six or eight months. I'd have to look it up to know for sure."

"We're gonna need to see her personnel file anyway," Magnell told her.

"No problem. Anything else?"

"Can you think of any other disgruntled employees, Meadow?" Pat asked.

"Nope. Like I said, Echo's a great boss."

"Well then, you can just point us in the direction of the employees' files and we'll look through them to see if we agree."

Meadow glared at Magnell before standing and turning to Pat. "The files are right this way. And if you need anything else, I'll be in my office the rest of the day."

"Thank you," Pat managed as she followed the swishing skirt into a back room.

❖

Kyla closed her eyes as the light seared through them. The throbbing in her head immediately worsened. She drew in as deep a breath as her sore sides would allow and slowly opened her eyes again.

She took in the sterile room and the muted whirring of machinery. More importantly she saw Echo, her partner of almost twenty years, dozing in a chair by her bed. Kyla tried to reposition herself but pain shot through her sides. As she groaned, Echo's eyes flew open.

"I'm sorry I woke you," Kyla whispered.

Echo leaned forward and took her hand. "Don't be. I'm sorry I fell asleep."

She stared at Echo. "Where's Colton?"

"He's fine, baby. He's staying with Sierra."

Sierra was Echo's sister who lived three blocks from

them. Her fourteen-year-old son, Levi, was Colton's age and the boys were inseparable.

"What happened?" Kyla asked. "Why am I here?"

"There was an accident."

"God, my head is so sore. And my sides…"

She stared down at the cast on her left leg. How could she not remember breaking her leg?

Echo stood and kissed her softly on the forehead. Looking into Kyla's eyes, she said, "We were kind of hoping you could tell *us* what happened."

"Tell you? Don't you know?"

Echo shook her head.

"Well, if you don't know, who does?"

"Right now, no one, really." Her gaze was intent. "You don't remember anything at all?"

Kyla shook her head. The action made her wince. "I remember a tree, that's all."

"They found the car at Lone Pine."

Kyla started to frown but the pain behind her eyes made her cringe. She touched her head. "Oh, my God. Did they shave my head?"

Echo stroked her hand soothingly. "They had to, baby. You have a…head injury."

That explained everything. The fuzziness. The sense that she had been awake but couldn't remember when or who she had talked to. "So, I have a concussion," Kyla murmured. "That's the problem."

Echo avoided her eyes. She seemed so tense Kyla wondered what she wasn't saying. "You need to rest. Dr. Gardner will explain everything again when she stops by this afternoon. Don't worry, kiddo. She's got your back."

Kyla grinned faintly at Echo's attempt to sound hip. Echo

still couldn't seem to grasp that she was forty-five years old. And now that their son was a teenager, she tried even harder to act like one herself.

"Dr. Gardner…" A cherubic face flashed into her mind. She recalled cute dimples and laughing green eyes.

"Curly blond hair. Quick smile. The Dr. Gardner we both have a crush on," Echo said with a trace of her usual humor.

Kyla studied her partner. Concern was apparent on her face, but there was more. Echo's normally warm eyes weren't. Her look was cool, almost detached. Her hair, always meticulously styled, stood in all different directions. Kyla felt like she was looking at a stranger. She felt a chasm between herself and the woman she loved, but she couldn't figure out why.

Echo had been Kyla's pillar for the past eighteen years. And Kyla had been hers. Theirs was a relationship of equals. She could always count on Echo to be there for her, just as Echo could count on her.

But something had changed. Kyla couldn't remember the previous week, but she could feel that something had happened to drive them apart. She struggled, cursing the obscurity that was once her memory. She could remember nothing but happy, content times with Echo and yet now she felt so disconnected, as if things hadn't been good between them for a very long time. Longer than just a week. She realized that relationships had their ups and downs, but Kyla sensed their downhill slide had lasted for so long that she doubted an uphill trend was in their future.

Their eyes met and she sensed something in Echo's gaze, a certain disquietude. Was she simply concerned about the injuries? Was she hiding something? What exactly wasn't Echo saying?

"Is there something you're not telling me?" Kyla asked.

Her eyes felt heavy. She could feel sleep approaching and tried to stay focused.

Something in Echo's voice tightened. "What do you mean?"

"The injuries…are they worse than you're letting on?"

"No. They're serious, but the doctors expect you to make a full recovery." Echo stroked her hand. "You're here and you're going to be back to normal in no time. That's all that matters."

Kyla closed her eyes. She felt exhausted and weak, and had trouble connecting her thoughts logically.

"Go to sleep, baby," Echo said. "Everything's okay."

Kyla wondered if she was imagining a guarded relief in Echo, as though she'd dodged a bullet. She heard the same tone whenever Echo tried to avoid an argument. Not one to back down if she knew she was right, Echo was quick to sidestep issues that might prove her in the wrong. Before Kyla could form another question, she felt herself slipping out of consciousness and decided not to fight it.

❖

"I'm just glad this is a small business," Pat said as she closed the last file. "Meadow was right. These give no indication that anyone here has any problem with Flannery."

"Of course, Flannery could have handled any situations off the record," Magnell countered.

"I don't know. Flannery strikes me as a by-the-books type. I'd imagine her documenting everything."

Magnell cast a sidelong glance her way, "Unless she doesn't want anyone to know about it. She's no fool, Pat."

"I honestly don't know how you see her as an evil genius."

He tossed Jenny Vasquez's file onto the desk.

"What? There's nothing in here."

"My point exactly."

"You think she should have documented an affair?"

"So you agree that she had one?"

"Not necessarily."

"Well, if she didn't, and this Vasquez woman was spreading rumors and making her life miserable, don't you think that might be mentioned in her exit interview?"

"Meadow conducted the exit interview. Maybe she didn't know how much to include."

Magnell poked his head out of the little room, "Hey, Meadow? Can you come here for a minute?"

He backed into the room as Meadow walked over and leaned against the door frame.

"Why didn't you give 'stalking the boss' as reason for dismissal?"

"Huh?"

"He's talking about your exit interview with Jenny Vasquez. You didn't say anything about the alleged affair. Why is that?"

She shrugged again. "Office gossip isn't usually valid as a reason for terminating employment."

Magnell opened Vasquez's file again. "Do you remember what reason you did give for firing her?"

"Sure. I told her she came to work late, left early, and took long lunches. It was hard to schedule classes not knowing when she'd be around."

Magnell nodded to his partner.

"Thanks, Meadow," she said.

When Meadow walked away, Magnell copied Jenny Vasquez's address into his notepad.

Pat checked her watch. "What are the chances she's home on a Saturday afternoon?"

"She was fired early December. Unless she's a trust-fund baby, she probably needs to work for a living, but maybe she takes weekends off, unlike some of us."

"If she has another job, it's not around here," Pat said.

"Why do you say that?"

Pat smiled. "How many gyms do you think are in Bidwell?"

"I see a lot of high-maintenance women in this town. You sure there isn't a gym on every corner?"

Pat laughed. "No, but along the lines of high maintenance, there are a few day spas. I wonder if she could have gotten a job at one of them."

"We're not going to find out anything standing around here."

CHAPTER THREE

G ood morning, Kyla," Dr. Gardner said. "And Echo. Nice to see you again."

Kyla looked into the voluptuous blonde's brilliant green eyes and smiled. Dr. Barbara Gardner was one of the cutest women she knew, and it amused her that Echo shared her opinion. Usually they disagreed on women, but Dr. Gardner was an exception. She'd been their primary physician for five years, and with her, they actually looked forward to appointments. She was full figured with wavy blond hair that framed her face. Her eyes sparkled all the time and her smile was contagious. As lousy as Kyla felt, she felt better seeing the good doctor.

"How are you feeling this morning, Kyla?"

"Better."

"Really?"

Kyla had to think for a minute. Did she feel better or was it just Dr. Gardner's presence that made a difference? "Comparatively speaking, of course. It would be hard to feel much worse."

"You have a point there." The doctor turned her attention to Kyla's medical chart. "Your fever is down. As is your blood pressure. Those are good signs. How is your head?"

"I hurt," Kyla replied honestly.

"What do you remember about last Friday night?"

"Not much." The room was fuzzy. It was hard to focus on the doctor. "How long have I been in here?"

"Four days."

"Are you joking?"

"I wish I was."

Kyla was stunned. Four days. Four days of lost time. She started to shake her head, but stopped at the pain. "That hurt. Note to self…don't shake head." She smiled weakly.

Dr. Gardner took her penlight from her pocket and shone it into Kyla's eyes. "On a scale of one to ten, how would you rate the pain in your head?"

"I'd say around a seven."

"Are you dizzy or nauseous or anything?"

"I feel a little queasy."

The doctor continued her questions, asking about Kyla's four broken ribs and her left leg, which was fractured below the knee.

"Am I gonna be okay, Doc?" Kyla asked, more worried about her head than her broken bones.

Dr. Gardner smiled. "I think you just might."

"Thank God." Echo's relief was transparent. "When do you think she'll be able to come home?"

"I'd say within the next couple of days, if the improvement is steady."

Echo sat back in her chair. She seemed almost disbelieving. "So we're out of the woods?"

"Just about. Outside of the pain, Kyla, how do you feel?"

"I'm not sure. I'll be happy to get out of this hospital." She hesitated. "Doc, how much do you know about what happened to me?"

As soon as she'd spoken, Kyla caught a look that passed

between Dr. Gardner and Echo, who shook her head almost imperceptibly. Dr. Gardner seemed reluctant to speak.

On a cautious note, she said, "Do you remember us talking about this a couple of days ago?"

Kyla searched her mind. She was certain no one had said a word to her about the accident, but Barbara Gardner obviously thought they'd had a conversation.

"I don't remember anything about that," she said. "I guess I wasn't all the way conscious."

"That could be a factor, but you may also have some minor short-term memory loss. It's pretty common among people who sustain brain trauma like yours."

"So I'll get my memory back?"

"The neurologist who read the MRIs assured me that your injuries aren't such that they would have caused permanent amnesia."

"So we *did* talk," Kyla mused aloud. "How weird. I can't remember that at all. What did you tell me?"

Another look passed between Echo and Dr. Gardner.

With professional calm, the doctor said, "Kyla, you were shot in the head—"

"Shot?" Kyla groaned instantly from the pain of her outburst.

"Kyla, I'm sure this can't be easy for you, but try to stay calm."

"Maybe this should wait," Echo said.

"No," Kyla whispered. "I need to know. Where was I when it happened?"

"You were found only a few blocks from your house," Dr. Gardner said. "The police haven't established the full circumstances. They're not sure where the shot occurred."

"The police," Kyla repeated. She could hardly take it in. Had someone discharged a weapon accidentally and she just had the bad luck to be in the wrong place at the wrong time? What were the odds of being hit by a stray bullet?

"They are treating this as a possible crime. That's why those detectives have been here a couple of times talking to you."

"I've talked to the police?" How was she going to cope once she got home if she couldn't remember anything at all? How would she do her job? "I don't believe this. It's like I have a complete blank. The last thing I can remember is being at work, but I don't know when that was."

"You suffered additional head injuries when your car rolled," Dr. Gardner continued. "That's when you broke your leg. And the airbag deployed, breaking a few ribs."

"I rolled the car?"

"Yes, ma'am. You went over the curb and rolled down that hill off Monroe Drive, where they're starting work on the Lone Pine development. The pine itself is what stopped the car."

"I got shot and wrecked my car?" Kyla managed a small, wry smile. "I guess I had a bad day, huh?"

"Since there were shots fired, the police had to be notified," Dr. Gardner said. "They're waiting for a full statement from you, when you're ready."

"But I don't remember anything. How can I give a statement?"

"I've told them there's been no change, but they want to verify that for themselves. I can tell them to come back tomorrow, if you like."

"You mean they're here?"

"Yes, just outside your room, getting in the way of the staff."

The doctor's tone was lighthearted but Kyla read between

the lines. If she spoke with them, they would leave. "I guess I should talk to them, then."

Dr. Gardner gave her a brief, grateful nod. "I've given explicit instructions that you are not to be harassed or taxed. They'll hear what you have to say and leave you alone. For now."

"For now?" Echo looked rattled. "They don't give up."

"If a crime was committed against Kyla, their job is to solve it," Dr. Gardner said softly.

Kyla blinked at the trace of censure in her tone. She had a point. If someone had deliberately shot at her, shouldn't they be happy to assist with the investigation? Kyla couldn't help but wonder what beef Echo had with the cops. She looked past the doctor to her partner, sensing she was upset. Maybe Echo wasn't angry with the detectives, maybe she was just suffering after days of stress and worry. This couldn't have been easy.

Trying to reassure her, Kyla said, "Don't worry. I don't mind seeing them."

"This amnesia won't last, Echo," Dr. Gardner added. "Kyla suffered a tremendous trauma, and she's been heavily sedated. Her memory might take time, but it will return." She lowered her gaze to Kyla, "And then you'll be able to tell the detectives exactly what happened on Friday night and they'll be able to do their job."

"I hope so. It will be better if I can remember, even if it's not pleasant."

Echo's smile looked forced, but Dr. Gardner gave Kyla an approving pat on the hand and said, "I'll show the detectives in."

❖

"Why do I have to leave?" Echo challenged the detectives.

"As I mentioned last time, it's standard procedure," the female detective replied politely. "We need to speak to Ms. Edmonds alone."

"Why? Can't you see she's been through a lot? She needs me here."

"We can't have her afraid to speak in front of others," the male detective said.

Kyla reminded herself of his name. Detective Magnell, and the woman next to him, with her long, dark hair pulled back in a tight bun, was Silverton.

"Why the hell would she be afraid to speak?" Echo retorted. "It's not like she can remember anything, anyway."

"She can tell us that," Detective Silverton said softly. "Please, you can wait in the hallway, Ms. Flannery. It shouldn't take long."

"I know it won't take long," Echo snapped as she stood. "Since all she can tell you, yet again, is that she doesn't know what happened."

"That's just the kind of thing we don't want her feeling pressured to say." Magnell again demonstrated his people skills.

"Kyla's a big girl." Echo's tone dripped with contempt. "She is her own person. And she's strong. No one can pressure her to do or say anything she doesn't want. Nobody." The last word was said meaningfully.

As soon as Echo departed, Detective Magnell turned his attention to Kyla.

"She's right, you know," Kyla whispered.

"About?"

"I don't remember anything."

"Maybe if you try a little harder."

"You're not known for your tact, are you?" Kyla remarked to the man looming over her.

Detective Silverton stepped closer to the bed and murmured something to him. He glared but moved grudgingly to one side to allow her to take over.

"It doesn't matter who asks me the question," Kyla said weakly. "The answer is the same. I can't remember anything."

"Let's try a different tack. What do you remember?"

"About Friday?"

"Yes. Do you remember being at work?"

Kyla thought hard before responding. "Yes. I remember work. It was a coworker's birthday."

Detective Magnell could not resist butting in. "Did you go out for drinks after work, then?"

"No." Kyla was rapidly losing patience for the large man with the shaved head. His blue eyes were beady and filled with suspicion, and she could feel the contempt radiating from him. "I don't drink with coworkers."

"Why's that?"

"It's just a policy I have. It's easy to get sucked into going out with them. You know, hanging out rather than going home. It could lead to neglecting my family. So I just don't do it."

Detective Silverton nodded. "Then the coworker's birthday is significant how?"

"I guess it's not," Kyla answered honestly. "It just happens to be what I remember about work that day."

"Okay." Silverton scribbled in her notebook. "Do you remember leaving work? The drive home?"

"The drive home? Let me think. I left work a little after five and got home just in time to take my son to his guitar lessons. Yeah, I do remember. Traffic was brutal."

"What do you do for a living?" Magnell asked.

"I'm a certified public accountant." She must have told them this before, but she supposed cops asked routine questions like this to put people at ease.

"A CPA? You sure you don't go drinking after work? I'd think you'd almost have to after crunching numbers all day. How boring."

Kyla rolled her eyes. "Not everyone is an adrenaline junkie, *Detective*."

Silverton flashed Magnell a look. Apparently Kyla wasn't the only one who found the man annoying.

"Where do you work?" Silverton asked.

"Leone. The firm's called Golden, Logan, and Jensen. It's just across from the Home Depot on Youngston Street."

"What time are your son's lessons?"

"From six to seven."

"Where did you pick Colton up to take him to the lesson on Friday?"

Kyla opened her mouth to answer automatically, then hesitated as she remembered she hadn't picked Colton up at home. She was puzzled. If he wasn't at home, getting ready, where was he? "I don't remember."

"Ah, come on." Magnell chimed in again. "You don't remember where your son was? Give me a break."

"Why don't you give *me* a break? You think I like having no idea how I got shot and smashed up my car?"

Detective Magnell made a sound that resembled a grunt.

"You don't remember picking him up." Detective Silverton persevered. "Do you remember dropping him off?"

Kyla rubbed her eyes in frustration. "I don't."

"Okay, Kyla. I promise this won't take much longer," Silverton continued. "Did you go home before you picked your son up?"

"I'm sorry. I just don't know."

"Not as sorry as we are," Magnell muttered, as if she were willfully obstructing a police inquiry.

"Does he have to be here?" Kyla asked Silverton.

"Unfortunately he does. Kyla, is there anything else you can tell us about Friday? Something that stuck in your mind?"

Kyla thought back to her usual morning coffee with Echo, followed by the morning commute. There was the usual office gossip session at the front desk, then just routine end-of-year work at her desk until the birthday cake was cut. "It was pretty normal. Nothing unusual."

As she said the words, a quick flash passed through her mind. Angry words. She wasn't sure who the speaker was. *Did you think you could get away with it?* A chill ran through Kyla's body. She tried to squeeze more detail from her mind, but she couldn't even put a face to the words. For all she knew, the accusation might have come from her. She had no idea what it meant or if it occurred on Friday. Perhaps some random thought had just popped into her head.

"Are you sure?" Detective Silverton's gaze was intent, her brown eyes the color of warm coffee. "I have the impression something occurred to you just then. What was it, Kyla?"

"I was just thinking about the accident," Kyla said.

For some reason she didn't want to repeat the words. First, they had to make sense. She needed to remember the context for them.

Before the detectives could ask another question, the door flew open and Dr. Gardner waltzed in.

"Enough," she proclaimed. "You've been in here pestering my patient for too long already. For God's sake, look at her. She's ashen. Clearly she can barely keep her eyes open."

Detective Magnell stood. "She looks fine to me."

Dr. Gardner wheeled around, hands on her hips. "And

how much medical training do you have? Never mind. I don't want to know. Session's over. Out you go."

"We really are almost through," Silverton argued.

"Correction. You *are* through. Good-bye, Detectives." Dr. Gardner's tone left no room for argument.

As the unlikely pair headed out the door, Magnell had to have the last word. Looking back over his shoulder, he said, "You better start thinking about who might want to blow your head off, lady."

CHAPTER FOUR

"Oh, it's you." Meadow hovered in the doorway of Echo's office, surprised to see her boss. "I thought you were at the hospital." She glanced down at a cardboard box on Echo's desk.

"I needed to pick up some paperwork." Echo placed her hand on the box, drawing the cardboard flaps closed.

"You should have told me. I'd have brought everything to you after work." Echo was always so reluctant to ask for help.

"You're already doing half my job for me," her boss said. "I don't need to drag you all over Bidwell to do my personal errands as well."

"I care about you. And Kyla."

"I know, and I really appreciate all you're doing." Echo leaned wearily against the desk. "It's been rough."

Meadow could see the toll the accident had taken. Echo's short brown hair needed a wash and her tan, chiseled face was unusually pale. Her blue eyes, usually so bright and lively, were shadowed with worry. Echo was a very attractive woman—tall and sinewy, standing close to six feet tall. Her strong jaw complemented her easy smile. And her dimples could make you melt. Confident and intelligent, she was quick with a joke, yet able to be serious when necessary. If she were single, Meadow would have wanted to date her. She had to admit, she'd felt jealous when she heard the gossip about Jenny Vasquez.

Echo had never shown a trace of interest in Meadow through the years they'd worked together, and Meadow had never had a problem with that. Echo was in a long-term relationship and was faithful to her partner. Meadow had actually admired that about her. Working in a gym, surrounded by hot women all the time, Echo had plenty of opportunity if she wanted to cheat on Kyla. Meadow wasn't blind. She knew women hit on her boss. But Echo never seemed to pay serious attention to any of them.

Jenny Vasquez was a different story. The minute she'd set foot in the door, Echo's behavior changed. Echo had always flirted briefly with the patrons that flirted with her. That was part of being a businesswoman. But employees had always seemed off-limits. Until Jenny arrived. Echo's face lit up and her blue eyes sparkled whenever Jenny walked in the door. It wasn't long after she was hired that the two started spending much of their time behind the closed door of Echo's office. Soon, Echo was spending less time at the gym. Jenny was conspicuously absent as well. Meadow couldn't remember who actually started the rumors of an affair between the women, but as soon as she heard it, she thought everything made sense.

"Is there anything I can do?" she offered. "If you need to go places, I could stay with her for a while."

Echo shook her head. "That's thoughtful of you, but as a matter of fact, Kyla's a lot better. She's coming home later today. That's why I'm here." Echo's smile seemed forced. "I thought I'd take a few hours to get organized."

"That's great news. I can't believe it's almost a week since the accident."

"It seems like forever," Echo said. "The longest six days of my life."

Meadow followed the motion of her hands as she secured the box with packaging tape. Her knuckles were white. "Did you find everything you need? After the cops were here, I tried to put all the records back where they belonged, but they made such a mess—"

"Are you saying the cops searched my office?"

"I'm sorry." Meadow knew her boss would hate the idea. She was particular about keeping gym records locked up to guard their clients' privacy. "They were pretty insistent. So I gave them the files to look through."

"You *what*?" Echo couldn't believe her ears. She railed at her assistant. "You gave the cops *what*? Why the fuck didn't call me, Meadow?"

"Why would I call you?" Meadow answered quietly, apparently unmoved by her boss's meltdown.

"Maybe because this is my fucking business!"

"Echo, it wasn't a big deal. They asked some questions and then looked at the files." She shrugged. "I don't know what you're getting all worked up over."

"Didn't you ever hear of a search warrant?" Echo snapped.

"Why would I care if they had a search warrant?"

"Well, for starters, they don't have the right to look through confidential files."

"What do we have to hide? Besides, what was I supposed to do?"

"You should have called me. I would have been here in two minutes *and* I would have insisted they get a search warrant."

"What are you hiding, Echo?"

Exasperated, Echo ran her hand over her short hair. "I'm

not hiding anything, Meadow. It's just a matter of rights. They violated ours. And you let them."

Meadow walked to the door of her boss's office. Before she left she said, "Don't go doing the whole civil rights violation routine on me. It won't work. If there's nothing you don't want them to find, there's no harm in their looking. If there is something, you've got bigger problems than I can imagine."

"I do have problems, Meadow. My partner was shot and has been lying in a hospital for almost a week. I'm about to bring her home and need to be able to take care of her without worrying about what's going on here at the gym."

"You don't need to worry about the business, Echo. If you're worried about something someone might find out, that's a completely different issue. And you're totally on your own with that."

❖

"Are you sure you're comfortable?" Echo asked for the millionth time.

"As comfortable as I can be," Kyla said. They'd been home for three hours and Echo still hadn't stopped fussing around her.

"Do you need something else? Water? An extra pillow?"

"How about a memory?"

Echo stopped fussing and stared at her. "Your face looks better," she offered.

Kyla gingerly felt her face. "I'm still swollen."

"True." Echo grinned. "But your bruises are more of a greenish color than the black and blue they started as."

"I appreciate you taking time off to stay with me, but it's really not necessary."

Kyla still couldn't remember anything about the night she

was shot and had an intense fear of being alone, but she was willing to try.

Echo sat on the bed and took her hand. "I feel horrible that I wasn't there to protect you. I'd do anything for you. I wish I could help you remember, baby. I'd give my eyeteeth to find who did this to you, and—"

"Do you think he'll come back?" Kyla blinked back tears.

"We don't know the circumstances, but whoever shot you probably doesn't know where you live," Echo answered.

"But he might."

"Not if it was random." Echo took a deep breath, but her voice was still shaky. "God, I wish I could have been there for you. I hate that I couldn't stop it."

"Oh, Echo. You couldn't have done anything."

"We don't know that. We don't even know what happened. But I promise you this, Kyla. You're safe now. No one's getting anywhere near you. Not while I'm around."

Kyla lay there, watching Echo. She seemed to be overdoing things, as though she had to make up for something. Normally, she was calm, cool, and collected. She seemed nervous, jittery. A memory from the hospital made its way into the forefront of her brain. The detectives had asked Echo a lot of questions when they thought Kyla was asleep. They seemed suspicious. On the other hand, they'd acted the same way when they talked to *her*, too. What did they think about the case? They were treating it as a crime. What did that mean?

Echo looked at her strangely. "Babe? What's up?"

"What do you mean?" Kyla tried to keep the edge out of her voice.

Echo climbed on the bed and crawled up to hold her. "You had the oddest expression on your face just then."

Kyla told herself she was being ridiculous. Echo loved

her. Obviously, she was making a fuss over her out of relief. She relaxed into Echo's embrace. "I'm sorry. It's just all so frustrating. I can't stand not remembering. And what if there's some danger? What about Colton?"

"You believe I'm here to protect you, don't you?"

"Of course." Try as she might to reassure herself, Kyla's doubts still lingered. The added fear was too much. She began to sob.

"It's okay, baby." Echo wiped away the tears. "We'll get through this."

Kyla cried harder at Echo's words. *Get through this?* What did Echo mean? That they'd work together to get Kyla healthy, mentally and physically? Or that they'd work through something else? Was everything okay between them? Kyla couldn't shake that phrase from her mind: *Did you think you could get away with it?* She still didn't know if she was the one who had asked that question, or if it was Echo, or even someone else.

"It's just so exasperating," she lamented. "I'm lying here with a shaved head and stitches. Not to mention a cast on my leg and taped ribs. And I don't remember how I ended up with any of it. Do you get that? You'd think a person would remember getting shot."

"You will, Kyla. Maybe it's just your mind protecting you."

"Who would want to shoot me, Echo? Who?"

"I've no idea, my love. No idea at all." Echo stood when she heard their son coming up the stairs.

"Hey, Moms." He strode across the room and kissed Kyla on the cheek. "You look beautiful."

"Give me a break."

He flashed her his winning smile. "To me, you look beautiful."

"You are such a smooth talker. You get that from her," Kyla had to smile. Echo possessed a silver tongue, and their son had inherited something of her charm. Kyla knew he adored her, though, and he probably did think she looked beautiful.

He flashed a dimpled grin Echo's way. "Hey, do you guys need me to hang out tonight? 'Cos I was gonna go hang with Montré tonight."

Montré was a member of one of the few black families in Bidwell. He and Colton had been fast friends since his family moved to town four years prior.

"What are you and Montré up to?"

"Levi's coming, too. We're gonna play video games. And spend the night. But I don't have to go. I mean, if you need me here—"

"No, that's fine. Do you need a ride?" Echo asked.

"Aunt Sierra said she'd drive me, if it's okay with you."

"That's fine."

Colton glanced lovingly at Kyla once more. "Seriously, you do look better."

Kyla beamed. "I couldn't look much worse."

"Well, that's true."

Echo laughed. This time Kyla and Colton joined her.

"You are so sweet," Kyla said.

"I try." Colton kissed both women on their cheeks before saying good night. "It's so good to have you home, Mom," he added sincerely.

"It's good to be home," Kyla said. "Have fun tonight."

"I will. See you guys tomorrow."

An awkward silence followed.

"He's such a good kid," Echo said.

"So you can see why I worry about his safety."

"I'm telling you—nothing's going to happen to him. Or you. You're both safe now. I promise you that."

Kyla stared at the handsome woman in front of her and had to wonder just how she could be so sure. If she hadn't had anything to do with all this, how could she promise they were safe? And was she really able to trust any promise Echo made?

❖

Echo's sleep was restless. She thought she'd sleep better with Kyla finally home. In actuality, she tossed and turned, worried that she might bump into her. She had just drifted off to sleep when Kyla's screaming woke her. Bolting upright, she stared as Kyla's face twisted in terror.

Not wanting to scare her, she patted her arm. "Kyla? Kyla. You're having a bad dream."

Kyla thrashed next to her and continued to scream, "No. No! Don't!"

"Kyla," Echo said more urgently as she lightly shook Kyla's arm. "Wake up, baby."

The thrashing subsided, Kyla stopped screaming but continued to mewl quietly. Her breathing was still rapid.

Torn between wanting to know what her lover might have glimpsed in her dreams and wanting her to sleep now that the terror had passed, Echo lay propped on an elbow and watched Kyla's breathing slowly return to normal. When Kyla was sleeping soundly again, Echo rolled onto her back and stared at the ceiling. Her stomach churned. She wondered when Kyla would start remembering, and what exactly she would remember. They'd quarreled on Friday, and it wasn't pretty. Would she remember that?

CHAPTER FIVE

Kyla felt groggy when she walked into the kitchen the next morning. She sat at the kitchen table and gratefully accepted the mug of coffee Echo handed her.

"I had the most awful nightmares last night."

"After what you've been through? I'd be surprised if you didn't have them."

"I suppose you're right. But this was like bits and pieces of horror movies flashing through my mind all night."

"It's a good thing it was all just a bad dream, huh?" Echo kissed her cheek as she walked past.

"Where are you going?" Kyla asked.

"I'm going downstairs to work out. Why?"

"Don't you even want to know what the dreams were about?"

Echo massaged her shoulders. "Baby, they were dreams, just your subconscious. Relax."

"You're awfully nonchalant."

"It's not nonchalance really. But okay, if you want to tell me, I'm all ears." Echo sat next to her.

"I'd hate to force you to take an interest."

"You're not forcing. Honest. I just don't want you

upsetting yourself." Echo paused. "And I don't think you can rely on dreams to explain anything."

The comment struck Kyla as odd. "I dreamt that we had a fight. It was brutal."

"Us? A brutal fight?" Echo's laugh sounded forced.

"It was just a brief flash. I don't even remember what it was about. And then there were gunshots."

Echo was suddenly attentive. "Gunshots? Because we fought?"

Kyla shook her head. "I don't know. But it wasn't me who was shot."

Echo relaxed again. "It wasn't you?"

"No. It was a little boy. I don't know him, and I didn't really see it. I just knew it happened. You know how dreams are. The next thing I knew I was falling into a dark hole and there was no bottom. That's when I woke up."

"Maybe you were dreaming about Colton, when he was little," Echo suggested. "You talked about him a lot in the hospital."

"Did I?"

"You were worried that he wasn't in the car when you crashed. You forgot that you hadn't picked him up that night."

"Yes." It seemed possible that the boy in her dreams was a manifestation of her fear that Colton could be hurt. Kyla was deeply thankful that he hadn't been in the car, but she was bewildered, too. Where was she, when she was meant to be picking up her son?

"I swear, in my dream I was screaming. I'm really surprised I didn't scream out loud and wake you up."

Echo changed the subject. She probably thought Kyla was getting herself worked up. "I tell you what, let me make you a bagel and then you can take some pain pills."

"Maybe if I didn't take so many pills, I'd start to remember something."

"Or maybe you'd just be in pain. You'll remember when you're ready."

"I'm ready now."

"Obviously you're not."

After breakfast, Kyla made herself comfortable in the bay window, with her leg elevated. She relaxed in the rare January sunshine while Echo went to the basement-turned-gym to work out.

❖

Exhausted and frustrated, Echo pushed herself hard, first on the treadmill and then with the weights. She'd been at it for forty-five minutes when she heard the doorbell ring. Swearing, she toweled off on the way to the door. Her mood darkened further when she saw the two detectives standing on the porch.

"What the hell do you want? She still doesn't remember anything. You gonna come by here every day, too?"

"If we have to," Magnell answered.

"We have a few more questions," Silverton said.

"Like what?"

"That's between your...*friend* and us," Magnell growled.

"Well, right now *I'm* between you and her, so you better lose the attitude."

Magnell drew himself up to his full height. "Are you trying to intimidate us?"

"I could ask you the same thing."

"You looking to be charged with obstructing justice?"

"Give me a break."

Pat Silverton stepped between the two. "Really, ma'am.

We just have a few questions. I give you my word that we won't be long."

Echo glared at Magnell a moment longer before stepping away from the doorway. She cringed at the thought of those two in her house.

"Kyla?" she called softly, leading the detectives into the living room.

"I heard," Kyla answered without looking away from the window.

Echo sat on the padded bench next to her. "Are you up for talking right now?"

Kyla placed her hand over Echo's and smiled weakly. "I have nothing to say, so I may as well say it now."

"You sure seem intent on her not talking to us," Magnell said. "Is there something you're afraid she'll say?"

"Please," Kyla said. "Can you two not fight? Please?"

"How are you feeling?" Pat Silverton's brown eyes seemed softer this visit.

"I'm getting there." Kyla wrapped her bathrobe tighter around herself.

"You look better."

"Thanks."

Magnell shot Echo a look. "We need to talk to her alone. If you'll excuse us."

"Actually, I won't excuse you. You wanna talk? Talk, but I'm not going anywhere."

Pat focused her gaze on Echo while speaking to Magnell, "You know, maybe she should stay. She could probably help."

"You can tell she controls Ms. Edmonds," Magnell noted.

Echo bolted to her feet. "I do not control Kyla. I told you before that she's her own person."

"Ms. Flannery," Pat soothed, "I'm sure she is. The thing is, there's always the chance of influence, which is why we interview adults alone. But since Kyla can't remember anything yet, we have other questions to ask, and I think you can help answer those."

Echo leaned her shoulder against the wall. "She needs her rest, so start asking."

Pat attempted to read something in Echo's eyes before giving up and turning her attention to Kyla. "I'm going to reword the question my partner threw out at the hospital. Can either of you think of anyone who'd want Ms. Edmonds dead?"

Kyla glanced at Echo.

"See?" Magnell ranted. "That's exactly why we want to interview her alone. She's scared to answer without consulting you first."

"I'm not afraid of anything," Kyla said. "Except maybe getting shot again."

"Well then, why don't you answer without looking to her for permission?"

"I didn't ask her for permission. Jesus, I'd hate to be your wife."

"No enemies?" Pat prompted. "Disgruntled clients?"

Kyla smiled wanly. "I'm a CPA. It's not a real dangerous occupation."

"No bitter ex-girlfriends or short-term intimate partners?"

"None. We've been together eighteen years."

"Impressive."

"Thanks."

"Apart from Colton, do you have any other children?"

"No."

"Any of his friends that might have issues with you?"

"He runs with a liberal crowd. I can't imagine any of them

doing anything like this. Do you really think it was someone I know?"

"That's hard to say. Could be. But not necessarily. But since you can't remember anything, we need to try to figure it out the hard way. First thing we want to do is rule out everyone we can."

"I wish I could help, but I really am a pretty unimposing person. Nonthreatening to my core. That goes for both of us. We're really not very intimidating."

Magnell looked Echo up and down, her muscular, sinewy form accentuated by her spandex shorts and sports bra.

Kyla followed his gaze and laughed. "Well, I said not very."

"What about parents of your kid's friends?" Magnell interjected, disdain apparent in his tone. "Any of them have issues with your lifestyle?"

"No, it's not like we flaunt our sexuality in their faces."

Magnell sneered and looked back at Echo. "Sometimes no flaunting is necessary."

Echo stepped toward him, but Pat moved between them. "What about your neighbors, Ms. Edmonds? Any problems with them?"

"Not a one. Some we get along with better than others, but there's nobody we have problems with."

"Who are you closest with?" Magnell asked.

"I'd say the Ponces. They live across the cul-de-sac. They're a good family. Four kids. Good Catholics."

"Good Catholics and they've got no problem with you two?"

"We're just people," Echo said.

"Yeah. Just keep telling yourself that."

"You never know when to shut up, do you?"

"And you? That's all you do. You stand there silently, not

offering any help. The only time you speak is to get in my face."

"Please. I'm sure Ms. Edmonds is getting tired," Pat said. "Just one more question for now. Ms. Flannery, do you ever drive Kyla's car?"

"Of course I do," Echo answered quickly.

"Often?"

"Sure. We drive each other's vehicles."

"I see." Magnell's ponderous tone implied there was something important about this information.

"You're saying if this was intentional, the target could have been either of us?" Kyla concluded softly.

"Do you think that's possible?" Pat asked.

"Are you saying someone might have been trying to kill Echo, and they got me instead?" Kyla was horrified.

"It seems more likely," Magnell said flatly. "Your friend has a more...colorful life than you."

"What do you mean?"

"You better ask her about that," he answered grimly.

Echo glared at him and Pat called the interview over. She handed Kyla her card. "If you can think of anything else that might help us, please give me a call."

Echo took the card from Kyla. "I'll put this over by the phone for you."

Kyla watched the three of them walk down the hall and couldn't help playing over Magnell's words. Echo really hadn't said much at the interviews. But maybe that was so they wouldn't think she was trying to coerce her. Or maybe she knew something. Maybe she knew something important.

She heard the front door close and Echo's footsteps descending to the basement. Amazed that her partner had gone straight back to her workout, Kyla held tightly to the rail as she made an uneasy trip down the steps to ask Echo what

Magnell was implying about her "colorful life." She paused on the bottom step and watched in dismay as Echo tossed the business card in the trash.

As quietly as she could, she crept back up to the living room, dragging her plaster-cast leg behind her. Her stomach knotted as she pondered what she'd just seen. Cold dread gripped her. Echo really didn't have any intention of helping. Why? She slumped into her favorite armchair and cradled her head. The pain meds must be making her paranoid. Echo wanted this nightmare to be over, too. And she'd promised to protect her.

Kyla wrapped her arms tightly around herself. What if it was Echo who needed protecting? Something was wrong. Something didn't make sense. If Echo was in danger, surely she would be falling over backward to help the detectives. The fact that she wasn't said a lot.

Kyla stared out the window. Maybe Echo was only trying to protect her. Maybe she believed if she kept the cops away from her, she'd protect Kyla from an ugly reality, Or maybe she didn't want Kyla to remember what happened. And if not, why? What was she hiding?

CHAPTER SIX

Y ou're different around those two," Tom Magnell said as Pat walked into the station. "What's going on?"

"Nothing's going on," Pat answered. "You're the one that seems to have a problem with them. Maybe I'm just trying to overcompensate."

Magnell sat at his desk in the new Bidwell police station. The red brick building with the charcoal rug and oversized wood desks were a far cry from the old metal desks and broken chairs that rolled on chipped linoleum at his old station. The fact that Bidwell had a total of eight cops explained why the place didn't feel crowded. Bidwell was nothing like the big city. Sometimes that was a good thing. During an attempted murder investigation, it was frustrating as hell.

"I don't have a problem with them," he said. "My gut instinct says they know more than they're saying. I think they're stonewalling."

Pat raised an eyebrow. "I don't think so. Let's face it. They're not used to dealing with the police. And that's not a bad thing. Plus, Edmonds has been shot. She's hurt, scared, and frustrated. Flannery is scared and frustrated, too. I'd say under the circumstances, their behavior is completely appropriate."

"There's nothing appropriate about their behavior," Magnell mumbled.

Pat stared at her partner. She took in the red and purple roadmap that covered the tip of his nose and wondered again how hard a drinker he was. And how that would affect his ability on the case. "Are you going to be able to continue on this case?"

"Of course. Why wouldn't I?"

"Do you think you can set your prejudices aside and investigate fairly?"

"I'm always fair," Magnell objected. He had shared his views with Pat on various occasions, pointing out that he'd seen bigots in all shapes and sizes on both sides of the law. Years in a big city had taught him that prejudice didn't belong on the police force, and as far as he was concerned, passing judgment based on race, creed, or color was strictly taboo. "And I'm not prejudiced. As a Christian, I know right from wrong. A man can't be faulted for that."

"That missing kid case is heating up," Pat referred to the disappearance of a six-year-old from southern Oregon the previous week. At first investigators had assumed the estranged father had kidnapped the boy, but his alibi had panned out. The guy was at work when his son was taken. He'd immediately offered to have his house searched and the cops found nothing. There was no evidence any child had been anywhere near the house in years.

"We caught the Edmonds shooting," Magnell said. "At least we've got a chance of clearing it. That underprivileged kid from Medford doesn't stand a chance. Give it another week and everyone will have forgotten him. He'll be yesterday's news."

"So, you believe odds are she was shot by someone she

knows." Pat did not want to hear his cold, heartless view of the kidnapped child.

"Yeah. Although the more I think about it, the more likely it seems the tall one was the intended vic."

"There you go again," Pat said. "Don't tell me you're not prejudiced. You assume Echo is the target because she's more stereotypically lesbian. She's a tall, confident, imposing woman. And you're prejudiced against her."

"Prejudiced? No. Suspicious? Yes."

Pat hoped her disgust wasn't apparent on her face. She'd faced prejudice since she was a kid. Having a cop for a dad had branded her an outcast with her peers, and being a lesbian branded her as such with society as a whole. People had always judged her without knowing her. She'd be damned if she'd sit back and let Magnell do that with these women. "If you're suspicious of her, how come you think she could have been the vic?"

"There are endless possibilities that need to be looked at in a murder investigation, Silverton. You can't just discount a possibility because you like the suspect. We have to consider that maybe she was supposed to get shot. Or, that she was the shooter."

"The bullet they found in the car was a thirty-eight caliber, which means the shooter couldn't have been too far away. He or she must have seen Edmonds before they shot."

"Not necessarily. It was just past six in the evening and she had her headlights on. The shooter wouldn't have seen her clearly through the windshield, even at forty miles an hour in the early evening darkness. He, or she, probably just got lucky. Fired at the silhouette."

"We can't find any record of a thirty-eight registered to Flannery. We don't even know if she can handle a gun."

"Then we better ask." Magnell proceeded to rattle off the facts as they knew them. "Edmonds took that bullet to the back left side of the head. The shot went through the driver's side window, which was down. And that's odd. And lends itself to the theory it was someone she knows. So the shooter could have been standing at her window talking to her before shooting her."

"And it happened not far from their house. This town doesn't have much of a crime rate. Random shootings aren't the norm, so it was probably a deliberate attempt on one of their lives."

Magnell nodded. "So we have to consider all the usual motives. Domestic violence. Grudge. Money."

"Flannery's alibi checks out."

Pat kept coming back to that flaw in Magnell's pet theory. Echo Flannery couldn't be in two places at once. It was possible that she could have conspired to have her partner shot and covered her own ass with a strong alibi. But if Flannery, not her partner, was actually the target, wouldn't the shooter have known that Flannery would be at work on a Friday evening?

"What's your point?" Magnell asked, as though he hadn't caught onto the logic.

This was unlikely, and Pat wondered if he was testing her. He seldom let her forget her rookie status versus his years of experience and the famous Magnell "gut instinct."

Trying not to sound sarcastic, she asked, "So what do we do now?"

"We go back to their lovely little slice of suburbia and ask their neighbors about them. See if anyone had issues. Get an unbiased opinion of what their family life is really like."

"I'll be surprised if we get any unbiased input," Pat muttered, following her partner back out to the car.

❖

Kyla sat in front of the monitor, staring at the words that showed up regardless of which Web site she visited. It was hard to pinpoint head trauma. It could be one thing. Or another. Cerebral spinal fluid could leak from her nose or mouth. She was thankful that wasn't happening. There were a lot of big, scary-sounding words that didn't seem to apply to her. She hadn't found anything about memory loss that explained how long it would last.

She stood up and stretched, working the kinks out of her neck as she watched the rain beating against the window. Deciding what she needed was a hot cup of tea, she limped toward the kitchen. She paused in the hallway when she heard Echo talking on the phone, clearly agitated at whoever was on the other end.

"I've told you not to call here," Echo ranted. "I've listened to what you have to say. Nothing is changing. Nothing. Do you understand?"

Kyla crept closer and peeped around the door.

"Seriously. Why? Why would I do anything to help you? You've caused enough harm to me and my family. Leave me alone. Don't call again. I mean that."

Echo was pacing. When she saw Kyla, she flushed and told the caller, "I have to go. This discussion is over."

"Is there a problem?" Kyla asked.

"How long have you been standing there?"

"Long enough." Kyla found herself transfixed by the pulse pounding in her lover's neck. "Who was it, Echo?"

"That's not important." Echo put her arm around Kyla and walked her into the kitchen. "What are you up to?"

Kyla hesitated, disturbed by Echo's evasiveness. "I was

looking up head injuries on the Internet. I don't have any of the other awful symptoms I've read about, but I can't remember shit, and I want to know why."

"I don't think it helps to pressure yourself this way. I wish you wouldn't be so impatient."

"Impatient? I think I've been the picture of patience."

Echo squeezed the water from a teabag and handed a cup to Kyla. "Why don't you rest for a while?"

"I can't. I need to find some answers." Kyla didn't understand why Echo couldn't grasp the frustration she was experiencing. It was almost like she didn't care. Either that or she didn't want Kyla to get her memory back. Which made Kyla even more determined to resume her search.

"We could always go see Dr. Gardner again," Echo suggested with a grin, but Kyla wasn't in the mood to engage in banter about the attractive doctor.

"I'll be upstairs. When you want to tell me who was on the phone, you're welcome to join me."

Kyla returned to the desk and sat down in front of her computer once more. She remembered Dr. Gardner saying something about post-traumatic stress disorder, so rather than looking up brain injuries that could result in amnesia, she typed "post traumatic amnesia." Several links took her to more Web sites that were too clinical for her. She didn't understand the jargon and just got more upset. She finally logged into an online dictionary and looked up the definition of amnesia. She read over and over that it meant partial or total memory loss. *Tell me something I don't know.*

Scrolling down, she saw that it could be induced by a "distressing or shocking experience." She couldn't help wondering if it was the shooting, the car crash, or something before the shooting that was distressing or shocking. One more search led her to a site that said amnesia was a primitive self-preservation mechanism, which comes into play when a person needs to protect herself from some form of severe emotional or physical trauma. The person subconsciously blocks out the pain of the emotional or physical trauma by burying the event so deeply there's no memory of what happened.

"Anything helpful?" Echo asked.

"I didn't hear you come in. I thought you'd gone to work."

"I said I'm not going back until next week. I wish I could help more."

"It would help to know who you were talking to on the phone."

"Why? What does it matter who I'm talking to?"

"It seems to matter to you."

Echo looked exasperated, "When did you get so paranoid?"

"I'm not paranoid. I heard you tell someone not to call you here. What am I supposed to think?"

Echo sat on the bed. "It was Jenny Vasquez. I don't know if you recall, I fired her from the gym." She looked awkward. "Do you remember her?"

How could Kyla forget? She frowned, puzzled that she could remember some things and not others. Rumors of an affair between Echo and that Vasquez woman had swirled the whole time she'd worked there. Echo had vehemently denied them, and Kyla had believed her. Had she been a fool? Was there more to the story than came to mind? Were there missing pieces? She couldn't ask Echo. If her behavior was any indication, she had something to hide.

"Why would she call here?" Kyla asked.

"She wants to come back to work at the gym. I keep telling her no. Meadow keeps telling her no. She started calling my cell, but I don't answer. So she called here."

"Why didn't you just tell me?"

"Because it's not your problem, and I don't want you getting upset over stupid things."

Kyla stared long and hard at the woman she'd lived with since college. The deep blue eyes that had always been pools of comfort seemed hard and cold. Her chiseled features were drawn and tight. A few weeks earlier, Kyla would have believed anything Echo said. Why doubt her now? Was her subconscious telling her something? Should she listen?

❖

"We might want to let them know we're talking to their neighbors," Pat said as her partner brought the unmarked Lincoln to a stop around the corner from Kyla and Echo's house.

He grunted his disagreement. "We don't have to ask anyone's permission to do our jobs. Besides, if they don't expect us to talk to their friends, they won't have had time to coach them."

"Coach them?" Pat rolled her eyes. "I don't know why you think they're such evil geniuses. Edmonds is still not doing all that great. I don't see her expending the energy necessary to coach anyone. And I don't see Flannery leaving her alone long enough to coach, either."

"You never know," came the response. "You can't give them too much credit."

Pat bit her tongue and followed Magnell's solid form to the house closest to the women's, a white Georgian colonial with a wide wraparound porch. She opened the screen and knocked on the paneled front door, surveying the rest of the neighborhood while they waited. It was quiet for a Friday afternoon near the end of the school day. Rain was coming down with a vengeance. She pulled her coat closer against the cold.

When the door finally opened, a small, elderly woman with frosted hair peered suspiciously through the screen. "Can I help you?"

They showed their badges.

"We'd like to ask you some questions." Magnell said.

The woman looked past them at their car, as if trying to ascertain if this was some sort of a hoax. "Questions about what?"

"Are you close to your neighbors?" Magnell tucked his badge into his jacket pocket.

"Some. What's this about?"

Pat answered before Magnell could. "Do you know that one of your neighbors was shot?"

The woman's hand flew to her mouth. Eyes wide, she asked, "When? Oh, good Lord. Was it a home invasion?"

"No ma'am. It happened a week ago."

The neighbor shook her head. "I've been out of town since Wednesday last week. I haven't had time to catch up on the gossip. Can you tell me who it is? Oh, dear. I do hope she's okay."

"She's improving every day. She should be fine. It's Kyla Edmonds."

The older woman shook her head. "That's just horrible."

Magnell, clearly frustrated at the social feel of the interview, asked, "Look, do you know anyone who might want to hurt either of them?"

"Oh, heavens no. I mean, their lifestyle isn't right, but no one around here would want to hurt them."

Magnell smiled smugly.

"Of course, I don't know them outside of the neighborhood."

"Of course." Magnell continued to smile as he handed her his card. "Thank you for your time, ma'am. If you happen to think of anything that might help us figure this out, you be sure to call, okay?"

Nobody answered at the next two houses, so Pat was relieved when a pregnant woman opened the door at the final house on the cul-de-sac. "What's going on?" she asked, pushing back long, red hair. A short, bald man walked up behind her.

After another display of badges, Pat inquired, "Are you aware that one of your neighbors was recently shot?"

"Of course," the woman responded. "Kyla Edmonds was shot last week. Does she remember anything yet?"

"Not yet," Pat answered.

"You close to those two?" Magnell asked.

"Sure," the woman answered.

"Not real, real close." The man behind her had his own thoughts. He stuck his hand out in Magnell's direction. "JT Ponce."

After prolonged competitive hand-pumping with Magnell, the handshake he gave Pat was weak and condescending.

The woman said, "I guess I'm closer than my husband is."

When Magnell's eyebrow shot up, Mr. Ponce immediately responded, "Not that close. She's not like that."

"Oh, please. Like what? I can be friends with them and not be like that." She continued, "He's so weird sometimes. Anyway, we go there for dinner. They come here. Their son babysits our kids. Like that. We're friendly enough."

"Do you know anyone who'd have any reason to hurt one of them?" Pat asked.

"Oh, no. No, no, no. They're good people. I can't imagine anyone wanting to hurt them."

"Well, they're not thugs or gangbangers or whatever," Mr. Ponce conceded.

Magnell held back a snort. Gangbangers in Bidwell. That'd be the day.

"Why don't you come in from the rain?" the woman offered. "Can I get you something to drink?"

Pat declined, but Magnell said, "I'd love a glass of water." The smugness on his face made her queasy. She wished she could reach out and wipe it off.

"So what's going on? Have you found out anything about Kyla's shooting?" Mrs. Ponce asked as she showed them into a beige living room.

"Well, you know how these things go," Magnell said. "There are lots of angles we need to look at."

"Are you following any leads more than others?"

"I have to admit," Magnell replied, crossing his leg over his knee and lacing his fingers behind his head, "this case is a tough one. She doesn't seem to remember anything. It's frustrating."

Mrs. Ponce plodded heavily into the adjoining kitchen and poured Magnell a glass of water. After handing it to him, she sat down on the sofa next to Pat. "Well, if there's anything we can do to help, we'd be happy to."

"We're really hoping to get some background on those two women," Magnell said. "Do they get along okay? Do they fight a lot?"

"Oh, no. They never fight," Mrs. Ponce said.

"Sure they fight," JT argued.

"You've never seen them fight," his wife challenged.

"They're two women. You know they fight." Magnell

exchanged a knowing look with the other male in the room. "I can't imagine that much estrogen in one house without some good catfights."

Pat seethed. The nerve. "Mrs. Ponce—"

"Please, call me Diane."

Pat smiled. "Thank you. So, Diane, you've never witnessed any animosity between them?"

"Animosity? Heavens no. They really are a great couple."

JT rolled his eyes.

"And you disagree why, Mr. Ponce?"

"First of all, in the Lord's eyes, they're not a couple, great or otherwise."

Over the sound of her own blood boiling, Pat heard Magnell say, "Amen to that."

"We're not here to pass judgment." Pat tried to keep her voice calm. "We're here to investigate a shooting. Why don't you tell us about their fighting?"

"Well, there was that Fourth of July party. You remember that, Di. There was a lot of drinking on their deck. Echo's whole family was there. I seem to recall tempers flying."

"Oh please, JT. You said yourself there was a lot of drinking. And the argument was between their extended family."

"I remember it getting awkward, with those two at each other's throats and us leaving early."

When Diane didn't respond, Magnell jumped in. "So they're big drinkers?"

"They've been known to party."

"Alcohol can make things ugly," Magnell declared with the sage authority of a cop who'd seen it all.

JT nodded. "Deviants are known for their drinking. Do you have any idea what the rate of alcoholism is among their type?"

"I'm telling you," Diane said, "they seem to get along just fine. Although, admittedly, we really don't see Echo around that much. Kyla's the one who's always in the yard or out talking to the neighbors. Echo keeps to herself."

"Makes you wonder if she's hiding something," Magnell said.

"We've heard yelling from the house." JT sounded pleased with himself. "Voices carry here. We often wonder what neighbors hear when we yell at our kids."

"Really? Can you make out what they say?"

"No," Diane replied. "Just raised voices."

"We're not the only ones," JT said. "Diane's a stay-at-home mom. She and the other moms talk."

Diane nodded. "I'm embarrassed to admit to gossiping, but several of us have heard those arguments."

"I'll need the names of those other moms you talk to," Magnell said.

"Oh, I'd hate to get anyone in trouble."

"You won't," Pat assured her. "We're just wanting information that might help with the investigation. Did you hear any fights the night of the shooting?"

"No. But I had the boys at a birthday party. So I wasn't home."

Pat nodded. "How about in the days just before the shooting?"

JT answered. "Yeah. I was picking up our mail and I heard both of them."

"When was that?" Magnell asked. "And did you hear what they were arguing about?"

"All I could make out was something about the gym and a woman named Jenny."

"There are three people living in that house," Pat pointed out. "Do you know which two were arguing?"

"It was women's voices."

"Yeah, they've got a teenage son," Magnell noted in a tone that suggested discomfort with this fact. Two mothers with a son? What was the world coming to? "Speaking of which, having a teenage son has got to add some stress to the equation."

"Have you met Colton?" Diane seemed almost amused. "He's such a good kid. He doesn't give them any trouble. He certainly doesn't stress them out."

"My wife likes to see the good in people," JT said.

"What about you?" Pat asked.

"I don't wear rose-colored glasses. I see people as they are."

Before she could respond, Magnell stood and handed them his card. "Thanks again for your time. If you think of anything else, be sure to call."

Before they left, Diane touched Pat's arm. "It's not like JT says," she whispered. "They're great together."

"Thank you." Pat said, forcing a smile.

❖

Echo sat at her desk in the master bedroom sipping tea and paying bills. She stopped with her mug halfway to her mouth when she saw the detectives walking back across the cul-de-sac. Her body tensed automatically, as if in preparation for the next knock on their door. Detective Silverton stared toward the house for a few seconds, unsmiling, before getting into the car.

"That was an interesting look," Kyla said, observing from beside the window.

They watched the detectives' car drive off.

"Why do you suppose they didn't come here?" Kyla asked.

"I don't know." Echo's calm seemed forced. "Maybe they saw enough of us this morning."

"I suppose they have to investigate close to home to see if anyone has a motive to hurt me."

"Yeah. I guess they have to be thorough."

"I wonder just how close they'll have to get to find their answers," Kyla threw over her shoulder as she left the room.

CHAPTER SEVEN

Pat Silverton knocked on the door of Jenny Vasquez's apartment, half expecting no answer. Most people weren't home on a Tuesday morning. She forced her jaw not to hit the floor when the door was answered by a gorgeous Latina. Her wavy black hair hung just past her shoulders, and her coal eyes glistened as she peered suspiciously at the detectives. Her full lips formed a seductive pout. She clearly hadn't been expecting company, dressed as she was in baggy gray sweats and a tight white tank top, which contrasted sharply with the large bronze breasts it clung to. Pat willed her eyes to move away from the hardened nipples clearly defined under her shirt.

"Jenny Vasquez?" she heard her partner ask. Good God. How could he speak? *Maybe he's not really human after all.*

"Who wants to know?" The woman's focus never left Pat's eyes.

Pat felt her skin heat under the brazen stare. She tried to look anywhere but at Vasquez.

"I'm Detective Magnell. This is my partner, Detective Silverton."

Pat's chest tightened when Vasquez licked her lips before she finally looked at the man speaking to her.

"And what do you want with me?" she looked back at Pat

and arched a perfectly shaped eyebrow. The slight accent that coated her words made her all the more alluring.

Finally finding her voice, Pat asked, "Do you mind if we come in?"

"Please do," Jenny purred and backed away from the door. "Don't mind the mess. The cleaning lady has the day off."

Pat looked around the tiny one-bedroom apartment. A flat-screen television hung from one wall of the front room they were in. A black leather couch lined the wall across from it. A matching recliner was situated next to the bar that separated the front room from the kitchen. The place was spotless.

"Detective Magnum?"

"Magnell," he corrected.

"Oh. Why don't you sit in the easy chair, and Detective Silverton and I can get comfortable on the couch."

Pat positioned herself against one arm of the couch. To her dismay, Vasquez sat inches from her. When she crossed her leg, it brushed against Pat's and electricity coursed through her veins. She knew she should move her leg, but she was paralyzed.

"Miss Vasquez," Magnell began. "It *is* 'Miss,' isn't it?"

"Oh, yes. I'm not taken." Jenny Vasquez swung her leg casually. Each graze caused Pat's crotch to clench.

"Miss Vasquez, we want to talk to you about Echo Flannery," Pat said, amazed her voice didn't crack.

Jenny straightened slightly and asked in a cold voice, "Why ask me about her?"

"We understand you used to work for her."

"And maybe more," Magnell added.

"Yes, she was my boss, and yes, we had an affair."

"Funny thing is, she says you didn't," Magnell said. "Have an affair, I mean."

"She lies."

"Why would she do that?" Pat asked.

"Because she lives the suburban dream. Living with her wife and kid in the Monroe neighborhood. If wifey-poo found out about me, she'd lose all that."

"Why didn't you tell Edmonds about this?" Magnell demanded.

"What's the point? Echo could have had me, but chose not to."

"I thought she did *have* you."

She glared across the room at him. "You know what I mean. She could have had more than an affair. We'd be together if she'd wanted it."

"So she called off your affair?" Pat asked.

"Yeah."

Magnell nodded like he'd already guessed this. "That must have pissed you off."

She twirled her hair around a finger while she thought. "It hurt. But it's her loss."

"It sounds like you want her back, Miss Vasquez," Pat said sympathetically. Exactly how hurt was Vasquez and what would she be willing to do to about it?

"If she wants to come back, she knows where to find me."

"I guess if her wife was out of the picture," Pat ignored Magnell's stare, "things might be different?"

"I doubt it."

"Why?"

"Look, I was a stray piece of ass to her."

"Are you sure that's all you were?"

"I want to believe otherwise. But it's easier if I think of it that way. I was her *puta*."

"So it's easier to think like that, but you know better, don't you?" Magnell challenged.

"It doesn't matter. We're not together. End of story."

"What's her relationship with Kyla like?" Pat changed the subject.

Jenny Vasquez rolled her eyes. "She's a controlling, ice-cold bitch."

Pat was careful not to let her surprise show. She hadn't gotten that feeling at all.

"Have you met her?"

"No. But I've seen her. She's so tight, she walks like she's holding a diamond between her butt cheeks."

"Where have you seen her?" Magnell asked.

"Around. You know. The store, the gym."

"So she works out at Echo's gym?" Pat asked.

"She doesn't work out often. Have you seen her?" Jenny allowed herself a soft chuckle before continuing, "But she'd stop by once in a while to rag on Echo."

"What would she rag on her about?"

Jenny lifted one shoulder. "Anything and everything. What wouldn't she rag about might be easier to answer."

"Maybe, but that wasn't the question," Magnell responded. "Why don't you give us an example of something specific?"

"I don't know. I just always heard her yelling at Echo. I don't know exactly what it was about."

"Well, I guess since she was always yelling, it's a good thing she only came around once in a while, huh?" Pat said. "I don't suppose you can be more specific about how often you saw her there?"

"Look, *querida,* most of the time that I worked in that place, Echo and I were here making love. So I only saw Kyla a few times. I couldn't tell you how often she actually came by, okay?"

"Fair enough," Magnell said. "And how long exactly did you 'work' there?"

"Eight months. From April to December."

"And how much of that was spent sleeping with your boss?"

Jenny grinned. "We started doing it in her office in May. By June, we spent most of our time here."

"Wasn't Echo worried that Kyla would stop by and catch the two of you?" Pat asked.

"I kept her a little too busy for worrying." Jenny smiled like the cat who'd just eaten the canary.

Pat had no doubt Jenny would be able to keep a woman's mind off anything but her. She was having a hard time staying focused on the task at hand herself. She met her partner's gaze and stood.

Jenny pouted up at her. "You have to leave so soon?"

"I think we have all we need for now," Magnell said.

Speak for yourself. Pat stared at Jenny's bottom lip and bit her own before coming to her senses and turning to the door. Magnell was halfway to the door when he stopped, staring into the bedroom.

"You like my bedroom, Detective? Sorry, you're not my type." Jenny switched her attention from Magnell to Pat, making a show of admiring her from head to toe.

"Actually, I was wondering about your e-mail."

"Why?"

"I just noticed your computer in there. I'm curious, did you and Echo ever exchange e-mails?"

"We exchanged a lot, Detective, but it was all in person."

"So no e-mails? Ever?"

"Maybe in the beginning. I don't remember."

"What were you doing between four and eight p.m. the Friday before last?" Pat asked. "The evening Ms. Flannery's partner was shot."

"I have no idea. It's what, ten days?"

"Eleven." To jog her memory, as they often did when trying to establish alibis, Pat added, "It was the same day as that seven-car pile-up caused by the guy who robbed the Dairy Queen."

"Sure, I remember that. I was applying for a job, then I went to the supermarket." Her eyes bored into Pat's. "You want an alibi, in other words?"

"That's what we do when we have to rule out suspects," Magnell said sarcastically. "We need names. Anyone who can verify your story."

"Is this the best you've got after eleven days?" Jenny laughed. "You think I shot her?"

"As my partner said, we have to rule you out. It's routine." Pat lifted her pen. "So can you give us those names?"

"I can do better than that." Jenny marched across the room and upended a messenger bag onto her coffee table. She fished through a pile of cards and receipts and found a slip of paper. She thrust it at Pat and said, "Here's the name of the guy who interviewed me and the office phone number. Call him."

"Oh, we will," Magnell promised. "And the supermarket?"

"How about investigating my fridge," Jenny invited angrily. "I only shop every two weeks. There's probably something in there from the deli. Those labels show a purchase date, don't they?"

Magnell looked at Pat.

"Yes, they show a date." Resigning herself, Pat followed Vasquez into the kitchen, awed by the firm ass that pushed against her baggy sweats.

Jenny knelt and dragged out the deli shelf. "I know I bought cheese that day." She handed Pat an assortment of sliced swiss and cheddar.

It took about ten seconds to find a label that confirmed a

5:45 p.m. alibi. The supermarket was at least twenty minutes from the shooting location. It was possible that she could have driven there in time to commit the crime, but the window was tight and how would she have known where Kyla would be? Would someone planning a shooting spend the hour leading up to the crime shopping for groceries? A smart criminal could be devious about setting up an alibi, but hotheaded Jenny Vasquez didn't seem organized enough to do that.

Pat photographed the cheese and asked, "Do you own a firearm, Miss Vasquez?"

Leaning against the fridge, her nipples jutting against the thin fabric of the top, Jenny said, "No. Are we done now?"

"For the moment, yes." Pat returned to the front door.

Magnell offered her his hand. "Thanks for your time, Miss Vasquez."

She reached instead for Pat's hand, which was at her side. "Thank *you*."

"If we need anything else from you, we'll get a hold of you." Pat quickly ended the handshake, disconcerted at the way her body reacted to Jenny's touch.

Her rapid withdrawal seemed to amuse the sexy Latina. "I look forward to it."

As the detectives left the apartment, Pat couldn't get the woman's body out of her mind. The pulsing between her legs continued and she had to remind herself it hadn't been a social call.

"I think we need to check her e-mail," Magnell said, interrupting her thoughts.

"I doubt she'll turn over her computer without a warrant. That'll take a few days. We don't have enough for an urgent request."

"If we have proof that Flannery was having an affair, not just hearsay, it will help us build the case against her."

He glanced over at Pat, who didn't respond. "Or maybe we'll find out that Vasquez is the one who wanted Edmonds dead. Look at her place. You gotta consider there's maybe a financial motive. She doesn't have the big house in Monroe Drive. She made a point about saying so."

Pat closed her eyes and absorbed the words. It was true Jenny Vasquez had sounded envious and resentful, and she was hot blooded. But was she impulsive enough and angry enough to attempt murder? Pat cautioned herself to keep her professional distance even as her own blood heated at the thought of seeing Jenny one more time.

❖

"What are you watching?" Echo asked as she folded herself onto the couch next to Kyla.

"Some stupid get-rich-quick infomercial."

Echo wrapped her arm around Kyla and pulled her close. She kissed the top of her head and asked, "You're starting to get cabin fever, aren't you?"

Kyla settled against her. "I really am. I'm so glad I'll be going back to work next week."

"I sure hope you're ready."

Kyla looked up at her. "I'm beyond ready. I can't stay in here hiding forever. Especially since I don't even know who I'm hiding from. I need to get back to the land of the living."

"Maybe what you need is a little mouth-to-mouth," Echo murmured, lowering her mouth to Kyla's.

The kiss was tender and loving, yet full of need. Kyla drew her closer and smiled into her eyes. "That was nice."

"It's been a long time, baby." Echo's hand settled on her jaw and she kissed her again.

"Too long," Kyla sighed.

She felt Echo's passion in return as she moved against her, their tongues dancing together. Her breathing got heavy as Echo leaned over her, her hand gliding softly over her whole body. Echo kissed her harder, her own heavy breathing testament to her arousal. Kyla pushed her hips toward her, needing more, craving contact with her woman. She felt Echo's hand slide down over her robe-covered breast, closing on it, sending shock waves to her soul. The tugging on the belt filled her with anticipation and relief. She wanted to be laid bare for her partner, to let Echo take her to places she'd forgotten existed, places where she could float freely and forget her problems.

Slowly, gently Echo kissed her cheek, up to her eyelids, stopping only when she got to the stitches above her eye. Kyla winced slightly, then took Echo's face in her hands and guided her mouth back to her own. Her body tingled as Echo's hand barely grazed over her bare skin to lovingly cup a breast. Her thumbs teased a nipple until it stood straight. Kyla lay still, reveling in the sensation. When she opened her eyes, she found Echo staring at her, her blue eyes dark with desire. The love she felt for this woman flooded Kyla, warming her from head to toe.

"Are you okay?" Echo whispered.

"I'm better than okay." Kyla ran her hands through Echo's thick dark brown hair.

Echo slowly, carefully kissed down Kyla's neck. As Kyla watched her mouth move closer to her nipple, it sank in how much she had missed intimacy with her partner. She was shocked to realize she wasn't sure how long it had been since they'd last made love. Months, perhaps. How had she been able to deny the urges her handsome partner stirred?

Kyla groaned and Echo lifted her head. "Was that a good groan or a bad groan?"

"Both," Kyla admitted.

Echo quickly slid off. "I'm sorry." She adjusted the robe to cover Kyla.

"Don't be." Kyla couldn't hide her dismay. She didn't want Echo to stop, and she was hurt by her sudden disengagement.

"I'll go get you some pills," Echo said. Her attention already seemed to be elsewhere.

Watching her walk off, Kyla struggled with conflicting emotions. A cloud of suspicion and doubt darkened her thoughts and she could feel her passion receding. Try as she might to hold on to the happiness she'd clung to just moments before, the feeling was gone, leaving her cold and confused.

CHAPTER EIGHT

Echo banged on Jenny's door again and resumed her pacing in the hallway. She was cursing her under her breath when the door finally opened and Jenny invited her in.

"You need to leave me the fuck alone," Echo told her as she strode across the threshold. "Don't ever call me again. Not at work. And especially not at home."

"Are you that afraid to have me come back to work for you?" Jenny purred.

"Afraid? What do you think?" Echo glared at her. "You're some kind of fucking nut job. I don't need you ruining my life or my business. Just stay the fuck away from me."

"Big tough Echo's afraid of me. I like that. You're afraid your wife is going to answer the phone if I call you, aren't you? How would you explain that?" Jenny stepped closer, her breasts centimeters from Echo.

Echo stepped back. "It doesn't matter. You're not going to call anymore, so that's not going to happen."

Jenny wouldn't be deterred. "You didn't even have the *cojones* to let me go yourself. Why don't you tell me right now why you had me fired?"

Exasperated, her face hot and sweat beading on her brow,

Echo stared disbelievingly. "You *know* why you were fired. Let it go. And don't ask again to come back."

Pulling the door open, she was surprised to see Detective Silverton standing on the other side. The detective quickly took in the look on Echo's face and cleared her throat.

"I'm sorry if I'm interrupting."

"You're not interrupting. I was just leaving." Echo squeezed between Silverton and the doorjamb.

Wondering what the detective was doing there, she chanced a backward glance when she was halfway down the hall. Silverton's gaze was trained on her, the expression cool and probing. What had Silverton concluded about the tension she'd just witnessed? Echo could kick herself for dropping in on Jenny. She should have known better. Without looking back again, she walked away as quickly as she could before the detective could ask any awkward questions. She had to calm down. If she got home in this state Kyla would start digging and she'd have to come up with an excuse for her mood. She cursed beneath her breath. Jenny always managed to get her so worked up.

Pat stared after Echo's receding back and tried to decide which of the unpleasant emotions grappling inside her would reign supreme. She had a case to investigate and knew better than to let her personal feelings interfere with her work. The fact that she had a hard time being professional around Jenny Vasquez aggravated her.

"Detective Silverton. What a pleasant surprise. Come in." Jenny seized Pat's hand and pulled her inside.

Pat's heart raced at the touch. The soft, warm hand on hers both comforted and aroused her. Disconcerted, she quickly slid out of the grip. "I'm here to see if you're going to assist us with our inquiries, Miss Vasquez. We'd like to see your laptop, if you don't mind."

"Oh, *querida*. I told you there's nothing on there. Now come, sit." Jenny patted the couch next to her.

Pat thought remaining on her feet was a better idea until Jenny leaned down to scratch her ankle. Her tank top, which had seemed so tight just moments before, fell away from her chest, leaving her full breasts bare for Pat's appreciation. Wiping her damp palms on her slacks, she accepted the invitation to sit.

Jenny moved closer to her on the couch, folding one leg under the other and turning to face Pat. Her arm rested on the back of the couch, close enough that Pat could feel the heat radiating from it. "Why are you so uptight, Detective? Surely you relax sometimes, don't you?" Her tongue slid across her full lips. Her smile was almost feral.

Pat questioned the logic of returning there alone. While Magnell was repulsive and frustrating to work with, at least he would have provided a buffer. "In my line of work, it's a little dangerous to relax on the job."

"Do you think I'm dangerous?" Jenny asked, moving even closer.

Abruptly, Pat stood. "About that laptop?"

"We'll get to that. Sit."

"Miss Vasquez, really. I'd think Ms. Flannery would have taken care of any needs you might have for the time being."

"Ms. Flannery? Echo? Take care of my needs?" Jenny burst out laughing. "That's the last thing she wanted."

"Please. I saw her when she left."

"And you thought... Oh, no. I told you before. We're through." Jenny stood and ran a hand along Pat's lapel. "Let's not talk about her anymore."

Looking into the pools of chocolate that were Jenny's eyes, Pat felt her resolve waver. Her chest burned where Jenny's hand rested. She was getting dizzy, her blood pounding in her ears. Jenny's lips parted and temptation called to Pat. She couldn't look away. Her legs felt heavy and a trickle of sweat rolled between her shoulder blades. As Jenny's hand slid around her neck, Pat came to her senses. Straightening up, she stepped back.

"I'm here for the computer. Not sloppy seconds."

"I told you, nothing is happening between her and me."

"She just happened to be leaving here first thing in the morning."

"Why are you so interested in us anyway?"

"So you admit there's an 'us'?"

"That's not what I meant."

"Look. You give me the computer and I'll stop asking questions and get out of your apartment."

"But what if I don't want you to go?"

"Either way, I'm going."

Jenny smiled. "If I say no, you have to go get a warrant and then come back, yes?"

"No. I get a warrant and my partner comes back to serve it," Pat said with what she hoped was coplike authority. "If you have nothing to hide about your relationship with Echo Flannery, then what's the problem?"

Jenny stared at her and seemed to be considering her options. Finally she went into the bedroom and came back with the laptop. "When will you bring it back?"

"As soon as I can."

"I can't wait."

Pat took one last look at Jenny and walked away before she could do or say anything she might regret.

❖

Kyla turned when she heard the front door slam.

"Baby?"

"It's me," Echo answered, storming into the kitchen.

Kyla's heart raced when she saw the anger in her partner's eyes.

"What, Echo? What is it?"

After a long hestiation, Echo burst out, "Those fucking cops think it's okay to visit the gym whenever they want and read through confidential files."

She seemed to be holding so much in, Kyla felt bad. "What on Earth would they want with your files?"

"I have no fucking clue."

"Sit." Kyla motioned to a bar stool. Echo collapsed on it, face in her hands. Kyla massaged her shoulders, her mind trying to wrap around what Echo was saying. "You're tense, baby. Relax."

"How can I relax? I feel violated."

"Maybe I watch too many cop shows, but how could they look at the files without a warrant?"

"They only need a warrant if I say they can't read them."

Kyla stopped mid-knead. "Okay, I'm confused."

"*Meadow* just handed everything over like they have a right to snoop through my life."

Kyla wasn't sure how to respond. Part of her felt sorry for Echo and agreed that Meadow had made a huge mistake. Part of her thought Echo was overreacting.

"Apparently they waltzed in, asked some questions, told her they wanted to see the files and she let them." Echo shook her head and turned to face her partner. "She didn't even call me. She should have known enough to pick up the phone."

"Not to be totally self-absorbed here, but I really don't understand what your employee files have to do with the person who shot me," Kyla said.

Echo stared at her blankly. "I didn't even think of that. I was just so pissed. But you're right. What do they think they'd learn from my files anyway?"

"And if they needed to talk to you, why not just come

here? Why go to your gym when you weren't there. Why talk to Meadow? Echo, this doesn't feel right."

Echo abandoned the bar stool and began pacing. "You know what else didn't feel right? Them sneaking over to the Ponces the other night. What the fuck could those people possibly know about the shooting?"

"I guess they have their reasons," Kyla said. "And I appreciate that they're out there doing what they can to solve this. I'm sure they'll get hold of me soon to let me know what's going on."

"Well, maybe we'd just better give them a call, since they don't seem to be in any hurry to call us. I want an explanation." She reached for the phone.

Kyla placed her hand over Echo's and said softly, "Baby, let me."

Echo's eyes hardened and Kyla moved her hand to her chest and patted it. "You know your temper. And it's fully flared right now. Besides, Detective Cro-Magnon thinks you don't allow me to think for myself. If you call to check, it'll reinforce that to him. Sit down. Have a glass of wine."

Echo sat at the table while Kyla called the station. She was obviously still fuming, rolling her eyes when Kyla's call was transferred and she left a message asking for one of the detectives to call her back.

"You should have asked specifically for Silverton," Echo chastised. "I don't think her sidekick is the considerate type."

"If there's anything to tell us, he can't keep it from us any more than she can. Now relax. We'll have our answers soon."

"I swear, I don't know how you stay so collected all the time," Echo said, pulling Kyla close and kissing her.

Instinctively, Kyla slid her arms around Echo's neck and held her, opening her mouth to welcome her partner's insistent tongue. Heat swept over her. Her whole body tingled until she unwillingly flashed back to Echo's anger about the files. Wouldn't Echo want the police to search whatever paperwork they wanted if it could help them find out who shot her? Why would she be mad about a bunch of files from the gym? Kyla could understand her being upset that she wasn't asked, but that was hardly the point. Someone had tried to kill her. It seemed pretty obvious that the detectives would have to start their search for clues close to home. Why was Echo so resentful? Shouldn't she be helping the investigation any way she could?

Kyla tried to push the unwelcome thoughts aside, but they persisted and Echo's kisses only made her uneasy. She had the feeling her partner was trying to distract her. It seemed like every time she started asking Echo questions, Echo avoided giving clear answers. Determined to keep herself grounded, she ended the kiss and pushed Echo away.

"What the hell?" Echo lashed out. "What was that all about?"

"I want to know what happened that Friday," Kyla said.

"How the hell should I know?" Echo answered, her red face showing her frustration. "You're the only one who can answer that question, babe. And you seem to have that buried deep inside."

Kyla shook her head. "No, I mean what happened between us?"

"What?" Echo sat down, apparently resigning herself to the discussion.

"Look, I know there has to be something. I don't remember, but I can *feel* it. There's something you're not telling me, Echo. I don't know what it is or even if it pertains to the shooting. Or the accident. But you're keeping it from me, and I have a right to know."

Echo ran her hands through her hair. "Just let me say

something." She hesitated. "I think you're being over-sensitive."

"Someone tried to kill me." Kyla formed each word carefully so she wouldn't scream them. "If I'm being 'over-sensitive,' I think I have good reason, don't you?"

Color rose in Echo's face. "Yes, you do."

"Then why would you keep information from me that might help me remember? Or don't you want me to remember?"

"Of *course* I want you to remember." Echo sighed heavily. "Kyla, we argued that evening. After all you've been through, I didn't see any need to have a postmortem about a stupid fight. It wasn't a big deal. We just had words like every other couple in the world."

"When? Did I see you before I picked up Colton?"

"No. We talked on the phone while you were on your way to get him."

"What was it about?"

"It's not important, babe. That's why I didn't say anything. It was a misunderstanding. We both got angry and it's probably just as well you don't remember it."

"Why not let me decide that? You still haven't told me what we were fighting about."

"Jenny," Echo responded tersely.

"Jenny Vasquez? I'm hearing that name way too much lately."

"I'm sorry. It's nothing I'm doing, I assure you."

"Why were we fighting about Jenny Vasquez?"

"Apparently she called you at work and said some pretty nasty things to you," Echo explained. "She blamed you for her getting fired."

"Why would she do that?"

"I have no idea." Echo sounded frustrated. "Ky, we went

through all this that night. I can't explain Jenny's behavior. She's not stable, so please don't take it out on me. Besides, it's not like she had anything to do with the shooting." The tone of her voice belied her confident words.

Kyla was astounded that they'd fought about this woman the night of the shooting, yet Echo had avoided mentioning that fact. "How can you be so sure she wasn't involved?"

It took a few seconds for Echo to reply. "I can't."

"Have you asked her?" When Echo didn't respond, Kyla said, "I take that as a no. Have you even told the detectives?"

"What would I say? You want me to accuse her?"

"Some nut job ex-employee of yours made a hostile phone call to me the night I was shot," Kyla responded angrily. "Even if you felt the need to protect me from the details, which I'm not convinced of, by the way. But even if you did, why would you hide this from the police? Are you protecting *her*?"

"Of course not, and I'll mention it to them if it'll make you happy. Look, I know this is hard on you." Echo placed her hands on Kyla's shoulders and tried to kiss her.

Kyla pulled away instantly. "You don't know the half of it. And it wouldn't be *as* hard if I felt I was getting even a little support from you."

"What more do you want from me? I'm here for you. I took time off work to take care of you. I've only just started back, and that's not full time." Echo stalked across to the window. She stood in silence, as though collecting herself, then said patiently, "I can't remember for you, Kyla. I would if I could. And I know you must feel very confused. But I can't explain what happened that night. I wasn't there."

"Someone else was, and they know what happened and why. If anybody knows who that someone might be, it would be really nice if they shared."

"Baby, please—"

"Please what? You have plenty to offer the detectives, if only you thought it important enough to do so. Instead, you're complaining to me about having your files looked at. Fuck, what a hassle. Your partner is shot, but how dare the cops dig around in your paperwork. I don't get it, Echo."

Her partner paled. "What are you saying?"

Kyla shrugged. "I'm saying you don't seem interested in getting to the bottom of this."

"That's crazy and you know it." Echo's eyes shone with tears. "I'm trying to put myself in your shoes. I'm trying to put your lack of trust in context. But babe, I've never been shot. I've never had amnesia, so it's a little hard. Please, put yourself in my shoes for a minute."

Kyla almost laughed out loud. Was Echo really trying to imply that *she* was being reasonable but Kyla was treating her unfairly? "I'm trying, Echo. But I'm having a hard time imagining withholding critical information in a criminal investigation."

"I'm sorry, I didn't think it was critical information."

Kyla just stared at her.

"I'm serious. I mean, I don't see Jenny as being capable of anything like this."

"You just said you can't be certain and she's unstable."

"Yes, but I didn't say she's criminally insane."

Kyla stared at her, hands on hips. "Don't you think that's something the detectives should decide?"

"I said I'll talk to them."

Kyla took in the statuesque form of her partner, shoulders down in dejection. Her expression was one of defeat and sorrow. Even so, her usual aura of confidence surrounded her and Kyla thought her more handsome than ever. How could she doubt Echo's intentions? Surely her mind was playing tricks on her. Maybe there was more to her uncertainty than the accident.

There was a distance between them, a lack of intimacy that wasn't new. Kyla couldn't remember the events surrounding the shooting, and she was even foggy on the months leading up to that night. But she knew one thing for certain: she and Echo hadn't been in step with each other for a long time. The air had gone out of their relationship so slowly she hadn't noticed at first. Then one evening, as they had dinner, she found herself recalling the passion and fascination Echo had always evoked in her, and wondering how those feelings could just evaporate. They knew each other so well, and took for granted so much, that they no longer had any reason to explore each other. The loss felt demoralizing and shocking, and she'd asked Echo that night if they could shake things up somehow.

Kyla recalled their conversation. It hadn't gone well. Echo seemed hurt. Kyla hadn't done a good job of explaining her fears. Instead she'd blamed Echo for choosing her business over her relationship. They'd ended up quarrelling. She didn't bring up the topic again in the months that followed, but she began noticing slights much more. If Echo was too busy to talk to her, she got pissy. When Echo came home late, she was cold toward her.

Often, in the months that followed, Kyla's thoughts would stray to her relationship and she would get angry that Echo seemed perfectly content to settle for the dull rut they were in. Kyla yearned for the closeness, the physical pleasures they hadn't shared in so long. She missed losing herself and giving herself, and letting her senses push her doubts away.

Impulsively, she closed the distance between them and slid her hands around Echo's neck. "Come here, lover," she whispered, running her hand through Echo's hair.

Echo seemed surprised. Relief softened her face. A tear spilled over. "I'm sorry I was being so stupid."

She bent and gently brushed Kyla's lips. She tried to stand

upright again, but Kyla wouldn't allow it. She kissed Echo, pressing her tongue to her lips, demanding entrance to her warm, moist mouth.

Echo turned her head away. "I'm not really in the mood."

Kyla held tight. "Echo, don't. I need this. *We* need this."

The look in Echo's eyes softened. She stroked Kyla's jaw and ran her thumb along her lips before dipping to taste them again. The kiss started soft and tender, but Kyla soon made it clear she wanted more. Her grip on Echo's head tightened, and she slid her tongue into Echo's mouth, sliding suggestively over hers.

Echo moaned, a deep guttural sound and frantically moved her tongue inside Kyla's mouth. They tightened their arms around each other, pressing their bodies together, raw electricity flowing between them. Kyla took Echo's hand and led her upstairs. Lying on the bed, she pulled her partner down with her and focused her gaze on Echo's. She took Echo's hand and placed it on her breast. She saw Echo's eyes cloud with passion just before she kissed her again, and she felt the need in her kiss.

Gingerly, she helped Echo get her shirt off and lay back down. Echo's hands roamed gently and lovingly over her body, carefully avoiding the sore, bruised areas, searing every inch she touched. Her hand slid under the waistband of Kyla's sweats, sending chills down her spine and making her nipples stand tall. Echo took one in her mouth as her hand slid lower, her fingers moving through Kyla's curls down to her swollen lips.

"Help me with these," Kyla whispered, trying to climb out of her sweats.

When she finally lay naked, completely exposed to her lover, she'd never felt safer in her life. Echo moved back to a hard nipple while her fingers slid inside Kyla's wet heat. Kyla spread her legs wider and moved her hand on top of Echo's. Together they moved in and out of her, deeper and deeper with each thrust.

Releasing her grip on Kyla's nipple, Echo trailed kisses and nibbles down her stomach. She carefully moved between Kyla's thighs and placed Kyla's leg over her shoulder as she finally took her in her mouth. Kyla rolled her hips as she felt Echo sucking on her lips. She wanted more, needed more. She felt Echo's tongue inside her and moved against her. She pressed Echo into her, craving the release that only Echo could give her. She was close, incredibly close, her body arching and thrusting.

The women moved together as only true lovers can. Each knowing what the other needed at that moment, they moved in sync as the white heat built in Kyla's soul. The explosion started at her very core. Heat flowed throughout her body until it all came together between her legs. She screamed her woman's name as the orgasms flooded her.

Lying completely satisfied in Echo's arms, Kyla wondered how she could ever have doubted her. She believed she could trust her with her life.

CHAPTER NINE

Kyla sat in front of the fire relaxing before the rest of her family arrived home for dinner. The sound of the rain beating on the roof was peaceful and she was determined to enjoy her last Friday before she had to go back to work. She sank into the overstuffed chair, rested her feet on the matching green ottoman, and absorbed the heat. She opened the paper and her eyes immediately went to the headline on the second page: SHOOTING VICTIM FROM BIDWELL IMPROVING. Below this was the line STILL NO SUSPECTS.

Kyla stared in disbelief. While she was well aware there wasn't always a lot of news worth printing in the small, weekly *Tri-Town Tribune*, which covered news pertinent to Bidwell, Gladden, and Fairview, she was still surprised to see her story in there. She didn't consider it newsworthy anymore, after two weeks.

The lights flickered as the wind picked up outside. Rain pelted the windows with greater intensity. The howling sent chills straight through her as she read the pathetic lack of details in the two-paragraph story. Feeling like she wasn't alone, she got up and closed the blinds, then checked all the locks downstairs. She sat down again but couldn't shake the eerie feeling that she was being watched. She scooted closer to the fire and read the article. She felt violated. It occurred to her that she hadn't read the papers from the time of the accident and she had no idea what was going on in the world around her. She didn't like seeing her name in print. The idea that anyone in the area could read about her repulsed her. She valued her privacy.

Seeing that Detective Magnell had been quoted really got her goat. How dared he speak to reporters on her behalf? There was no mention of Detective Silverton at all. Somehow comments from the female detective would have been easier to take. The article also said that Echo Flannery had declined to comment and that Kyla couldn't be reached. Suspicion crept back, causing her to wonder why Echo wouldn't let her talk to the reporters.

Her neighborhood, Monroe, was mentioned in the next paragraph, sending chills through her body. A flash of lightning lit the room and was followed by darkness as the lights went out. Kyla carefully toed her way to the hearth, lit some candles, then sank back into her chair. A cold fist of dread formed in the pit of her stomach as she realized that, assuming Echo was innocent, whoever had shot her now knew which neighborhood she lived in and the name of her partner, and even the name of Echo's business. Deep in her heart she believed it was a stranger who'd shot her. Who might have thought she was dead. Who now knew her name and that she was alive, and who could get her address from the telephone directory.

The creak of the front door opening caused her heart to jump to her throat. "This storm is brutal," Echo called from the entryway.

"Thank God," Kyla whispered.

Echo's shadow loomed in the glow of the candlelight. She

immediately scooped Kyla in her arms and held her until her crying died down. "Kyla, baby. What's going on?"

She took the paper Kyla handed to her and skimmed the article.

"Why didn't you tell me reporters were calling?"

"I didn't think you needed to be disturbed. You know how the media can be."

"Actually, I don't."

Echo hugged her closer. "And it was my goal to keep it that way. They have no right to harass us. You're the victim here."

"Anyone who reads that paper will know I live in this neighborhood. Doesn't that even worry you? Whoever shot me now knows I'm alive and where I live!"

Echo skimmed the article again. Her whole body tensed and she held Kyla closer. "Whoever did this isn't going to hang around with the police all over the case and parked in the neighborhood all the time. Besides, your name has been in the papers from the start. If anyone was going to come looking for you, it would have happened by now."

Kyla shuddered. "We don't know that. I feel like someone's watching me. Maybe he's just waiting for things to die down."

"No one's watching." Echo kissed the top of her head. "No one's going to get you, baby. Not while I'm here. I'll keep you safe. I promise."

Kyla burrowed deeper against her and Echo absently rubbed her back while she stared into the darkness. Echo seemed very certain that she wasn't in danger from some stalker. How could she be so blasé? Kyla thought about the detectives again and about Echo's attitude toward the investigation. Since their lovemaking, she'd felt closer to her and had started to believe

Echo was just as confused and upset as she was. She'd started to hope the crisis would draw them closer together. Yet at other times, all her doubts crept back in and she wondered if Echo even wanted their relationship anymore. She wished she knew.

❖

"Any news on the laptop?" Pat asked as she dropped her coat over the back of her chair.

"Not yet." Magnell looked up from the papers on his desk. He was bleary-eyed, not unusual for a Monday morning after a weekend glued to the sports network. "Anything else from the Flannery woman?"

Pat had been dispatched to ask Echo why she was at Vasquez's apartment that day. Echo had all but told her to go fuck herself. "She's not exactly cooperative," Pat said, collapsing in her chair. "I can't decide if she's hedging for personal reasons or if there's a link."

"You said Flannery was all flushed and sweaty when you saw her." Magnell huffed. "No doubt what was going on there, so she's still carrying on with this Vasquez woman. What does that tell you?"

"We don't have anything concrete," Pat reminded him. "And they both have alibis for the shooting."

"The timeline has plenty of wiggle room," Magnell said. "Vasquez can't prove where she went after the supermarket."

"No firearm registration," Pat said.

"No shit. So she bought one illegally."

"It's not as easy as that," Pat said. "They don't sell them on Craigslist."

Magnell shrugged. "I still like Flannery for it. We need to keep the pressure on both of them till something gives."

"I don't know." Pat couldn't share his enthusiasm. "I keep wondering if there's something we're not seeing."

She hesitated to state her thoughts. Magnell had been doing this a whole lot longer than she had. But she was uneasy with the assumptions being made. Almost from the start he'd only wanted to focus on the one line of inquiry, with Echo Flannery in his sights as the best potential suspect. Pat didn't want to start making facts fit the theory. Their case would fall apart in court unless it was bulletproof, and they didn't have a shred of real evidence so far.

She was less than thrilled to find that Echo and Jenny were still sleeping together, and she wasn't completely comfortable with her own dismay. It was crazy to let herself lust after a potential suspect, but her mind kept returning to Jenny Vasquez and her body kept reacting. Proof of the affair definitively marked Jenny as off-limits, and Pat was too committed to her work to make a stupid mistake like asking Jenny to have a drink with her. But she was tempted, and that disturbed her. She wasn't sure if she was the one making facts fit a theory, trying to prove Jenny had nothing to do with the shooting.

Even if they cleared her, and even if Echo's infidelity had nothing to do with the crime, Pat would be making a big mistake if she saw Jenny in a social situation until they'd made an arrest.

"What's up with you?" Magnell broke in on her thoughts. "You should be bouncing off the wall after stumbling on that little scenario. The two of them together like that. What the heck were they thinking?"

"If they're guilty of something, it certainly wouldn't make much sense to see each other," Pat replied.

"Yeah, right, criminals are always so damned smart about that stuff." Magnell snorted. "These two are having an affair, and if they cooked this up between them, they've got plenty to talk about since Edmonds is still alive, and it's only a matter of time till she remembers something. So cheer up. They'll make a mistake. We just have to keep pushing."

Pat forced herself to focus. "You're right. So maybe we need to do something with this information that won't be too pleasant."

"You mean confronting Flannery?" Magnell grinned. "Well, that could certainly add a twist to things."

"Actually, I was thinking more about Edmonds."

"Edmonds? Why?"

Pat questioned her own motives again. Was there a professional reason, or did she simply feel Kyla should know what her partner was up to? "Maybe it would shake things up," she said. "It just feels like she should know that we're investigating her partner and she should be careful."

"I don't see how that's going to help us out. I mean, sure Flannery's a rat, and Edmonds should watch her back, but maybe she'll just walk away, then what? They get what they want if she's out of the picture, so they'll close ranks and we'll get zip."

"Or maybe she'll confront Echo and the truth will come out," Pat said.

"Good point." Magnell paused. "You know, if we tell Edmonds, maybe it'll jog her memory. Cause some flashbacks or something."

"Possibly."

"Really, it can only help." Magnell stood up and put his coat on. "Let's go see what Edmonds knows about the affair, and how she takes it when she finds out they're still doing the deed. Or whatever those people call it."

Pat was too disgusted to comment as she followed him

out to the car and rode in silence the twelve miles to Kyla's office.

"You ready for the fireworks?" Magnell asked, getting out of the car.

"Not exactly," Pat mumbled under her breath.

"Well, get ready." Magnell walked to the door, leaving Pat straggling behind him.

Once at the front desk, he reached for his badge, but Pat stopped him. There was no need to alert everyone that they were cops. "Is Kyla Edmonds here?" she asked.

"She is," the perky receptionist answered. "May I tell her who's asking for her?"

"Tell her Pat Silverton."

A few seconds later Kyla emerged from a short hallway. She looked annoyed. "Why are you here?"

"Is there somewhere we can talk?" Pat asked.

"We can talk here, since that seems to be what you want," Kyla plunked herself down in a chair in the reception area. "Well? Is there some news?"

"Maybe, but you don't want to discuss this in front of these people," Magnell said. "You got an office or something?"

"All my colleagues know I was shot. They know there's an investigation. If you wanted secrecy you should have come by my house, later."

"We wanted to speak with you alone," Pat said gently.

"Without Ms. Flannery," Magnell added significantly.

Kyla sighed, not in the mood to play games. "Fine."

She led the detectives to her office and closed the door. When she was seated behind her desk, she asked again, "What is it you want to talk about?"

Magnell looked at his partner who stared at the floor. He took the lead, "Have you ever heard of Jenny Vasquez?"

"Of course I've heard of her. Why?"

"In what capacity?"

"What do you mean?"

"He means how do you know her?" Pat Silverton said.

Kyla was growing less comfortable by the moment. "She used to work for Echo. Why are you asking me about her?"

"She worked for her? That was it? Or was there more?"

"*More*? Their relationship was strictly that of employer and employee."

"Has Miss Vasquez ever come by your house?"

Kyla's heart raced. She did not like this line of questioning. Had Jenny ever been to their house? God, she hoped not.

"Kyla?" Silverton prodded.

"No. She's never been to our house."

"When was the last time Echo had contact with her?"

Something in Detective Silverton's gaze made Kyla flinch. She was used to sympathy in the faces of the people around her, but not the pity that flashed from the detective's soft brown eyes. "I don't see the point of all these questions."

"Why not let us decide that?" Magnell interjected.

"Fine. As far as I know, they haven't had contact for months."

"You sure?"

Before she laid into the overbearing man, Kyla's memory landed on the phone call she'd overheard recently. "Actually, I know they spoke on the phone last week."

"Really?"

Silverton cast him a warning glance before asking, "Do you know what that was about?"

"Echo told me Jenny wanted her job back."

"And you believe her?"

Trying to ignore the gnawing in her belly, Kyla answered, "Why wouldn't I?"

Detective Silverton leaned forward in her chair, her focus intent. Softly she said, "There's really no delicate way to put this, Kyla. So I'm just going to say it. Have you ever heard anything about a possible affair between them?"

Kyla thought she'd be sick. Worries and doubts flooded over her, but she forced herself to answer. "There were rumors. Echo told me people had been talking. But I never believed them."

"Why not?" Magnell asked.

"To be honest, I had no reason to believe them. Echo and I have a very healthy relationship." She hoped she sounded more confident about that than she felt.

"So as far as you know," Silverton continued, "they're not still in contact in any capacity. With the exception of the recent phone call."

"That's correct."

Magnell leaned back in his seat and said, "So you'd find it interesting that Flannery was at Miss Vasquez's home one day last week when we called by to ask a few routine questions?"

Negative emotions raged inside Kyla. She sat silently, trying to absorb the information.

Magnell said to Silverton, "Tell her how she looked."

Silverton cleared her throat. "Echo was flushed and appeared to be perspiring. She was very surprised to see us. Did she happen to mention that she'd run into us? And where?"

Kyla shook her head and wondered how much more she'd be forced to deal with. Wasn't the shooting enough? Now this? Or were they all connected? What exactly were they trying to imply? She knew almost before she asked, "What are you getting at?"

"We need to ascertain how much you know about their relationship," Pat said. Her tone was gentle and that look was in her eyes again. "Kyla, we're just doing our job, trying to find out who hurt you. We have to go where the facts lead us."

And they led to Echo? Having had just about all she could take, Kyla gave up trying to control her emotions. She felt her eyes watering and heard her voice shake when she demanded, "Are you saying Echo is a suspect in the shooting?"

Magnell answered, "We need to examine every angle right now."

Kyla rolled her eyes. "What about Jenny? Is she a suspect? Are you investigating her?"

"Again, ma'am, we can't rule anything out yet."

The detectives stood and Kyla took the card Silverton handed her.

"Please call us if you remember anything at all that might help," Silverton said. "In the meantime, we'll be in touch."

Kyla buried her face in her hands as soon as they left. She was strong, always had been. But she'd grown used to relying on Echo for extra strength over the years, and now that she needed her most, she didn't know if she could trust her. She had no one to turn to. She had never felt so alone in her life.

❖

Kyla stood exhausted in front of the house after her colleague dropped her off. Her first day back to work had been much more draining than she'd anticipated. Her unexpected visitors hadn't helped. All she wanted was a hot bath followed by a warm bed. Or maybe just a nap right where she sat. Steeling herself for the inevitable confrontation, she grabbed her briefcase, balanced on her crutches, and made herself hobble toward the house. She would be thankful to get the cast off her leg in a few weeks and be able to drive again.

As she opened the door to the house, her nose was greeted

by a cacophony of aromas. She closed her eyes and inhaled. Her stomach grumbled, making her painfully aware that she hadn't eaten all day. She followed the tantalizing smells to their source, where she found Colton stirring a pot on the stove and Echo standing next to him, offering instructions. Kyla stood quietly for a moment, taking in the scene. She'd always considered herself lucky to have those two in her life. The foundation of her life had always been her family. She felt that foundation crumbling

She tried to conjure up the contentment she always felt at mealtimes with the two people who mattered most in her world, but all she could conjure up was suspicion. Had Echo put this family moment together out of guilt? "I'd be afraid seeing you two like that if the house didn't smell so good."

Colton looked up from his cooking and grinned, showing off a deep dimple in his cheek.

Echo crossed the room, took her briefcase, and tried to kiss her. Kyla pulled away.

"You look tired," Echo said, apparently not chagrined.

"Gee, thanks."

"Seriously. Sit. How'd it go today?"

Kyla didn't argue. She sat down and gratefully accepted the glass of Malbec that Echo handed her. "Seriously? It was long."

And it was only going to get longer. She was torn between relief that Colton was there and frustration that her conversation with Echo had to wait.

"Hey," Colton said over his shoulder. "Are you supposed to be drinking? I mean, you're on pain pills and all."

"I haven't had a pain pill all day and I promise not to have one tonight, okay?"

"You really don't think you need one?" he asked.

"I don't. Why?"

"That's awesome." He favored her with a bright smile, relief showing on his young face.

Echo tousled his blond hair. "Yes, it is."

Kyla walked over and hugged their son. "I love you, Colton."

"I love you, Mom." He looked at Echo. "Both of you."

"You don't need to worry about me, kiddo. I'm healing just fine."

"I have to worry."

"Why?"

"Because when I let my guard down for a minute, you go and get shot and wreck the car. My car, by the way. Or what would have been."

"You're lucky you're cute," Echo told him.

"So you've said." He laughed. "Now go relax, Mom. Dinner's almost ready."

Kyla wished she could relax. She sat sipping her wine and watching them, wondering how Echo could be so duplicitous. For Colton's sake, she tried to act like she enjoyed the meal. They had made her favorite Greek pork dish, *hirino ladorigani*. They normally stuck to a vegetarian diet, so the meat was a special treat. A treat that fueled Kyla's suspicion.

"This is fantastic," she lied, forcing a smile at her son. "Thank you so much."

"You needed something special." Echo reached for her free hand across the table. "And this is just the start. I want to make you feel good."

An unwelcome thought niggled at the back of Kyla's brain. What if Echo was trying to seduce her to allay suspicion? Since their lovemaking the previous week, she'd been affectionate and sweet. In her arms, it was so easy to forget everything. But how could Kyla forget her problems if she was with Echo?

Echo herself was a problem. Kyla couldn't trust her, much less allow her to make love to her. That wasn't going to happen again. It was time for answers.

She withdrew her hand. "I really do appreciate it. But I'll tell you, between the wine, the meal, and my day, I'll sleep like a baby tonight."

Kyla glanced at Echo, who refused to meet her gaze, furthering Kyla's suspicion that her partner was hiding something from her.

❖

Kyla lay staring at the ceiling, recalling the events of the day. She was exhausted but doubted she'd be able to sleep. It wasn't likely that her brain would slow down anytime soon. She was surprised when she woke to the feel of Echo's arm around her, pulling her close.

She turned to face her. "When was the last time you saw Jenny?"

"Baby, we've already had this discussion."

"Please answer me."

"I told you she's not important," Echo began.

I know you've seen her, just tell me why."

"I don't know what you're talking about."

"Whatever, Echo. I know you were at Jenny's last week." With the only light being the moonbeams filtered through the blinds, Kyla could still make out the tightening of Echo's jaw. "At least you didn't deny it."

"Kyla, I can explain."

"Sure you can. I'm tired of the lies, Echo. So please just tell me what's going on."

"I didn't want to upset you."

"Upset me? You think I would be upset that you were at your girlfriend's apartment? Why the hell would that upset me?"

"She's not my girlfriend." Echo reached for her again.

Kyla got out of the bed. "The hell she's not. I tried to ignore the rumors. I was sure you wouldn't do that to me. To us. To Colton. But I know better now. I can't believe I let you play me like that. God, I've been a fool."

"For Christ's sake, Kyla. It's not how it looks."

"It never is," Kyla replied, grabbing her blanket and yanking the comforter off the bed.

"Where are you going?" The panic was evident in Echo's voice.

"I'm sleeping in the guest room," Kyla said as she started toward the door. "I can't sleep in here. And I can't help but wonder, if you're capable of cheating on me, what else are you capable of?"

CHAPTER TEN

K yla and Echo sat downstairs watching television in silence. They'd barely spoken since their quarrel over Jenny the night before. When the tension got to be too much, Kyla went upstairs to try to rest. She lay down and closed her eyes, but sleep escaped her. Instead, the feeling of fear kept washing over her, making her heart race and leaving her unable to relax. While no specifics of that night came back to her, no details took shape, she was still left with an overwhelming sense of fear. As if she were still in danger.

Driven by an unknown need, she got out of bed and took Colton's photo albums out of an old oak trunk they kept at the foot of the bed. She sat on their king-size bed and looked through them. Starting when Colton was a newborn, she took a photographic tour through her son's early years. By the time she reached Colton's first elementary school days, tears were streaming down her face. She moved her fingers over the covered photos, imagining stroking the soft, young face that smiled back at her.

She didn't look up when Echo entered the room carrying a cup of chamomile tea. "This should calm your nerves," she said as she approached the bed. "What are you looking at?"

"Memories."

Echo set the cup on the nightstand. "We have to talk."

"I think I've heard enough."

"You're leaping to conclusions. If you could remember what happened, you'd know the cops are nuts investigating me and that crazy bitch Jenny. Please think, Kyla." Echo took her by the shoulders and held her gaze. "Please. You know who I am. I would never hurt you."

It was hard not to fall into the tenderness of her stare and the sheer beauty of her. If anything, Echo was even more attractive than she'd been when they first met. Kyla's heart thumped hard as she watched Echo's mouth softly part and her eyes start to warm. The fingers on Kyla's shoulder fell away, leaving her bereft and longing for more. She stared down at the floor, struggling with a yearning so powerful it made her hands tremble.

She wanted the Echo she'd fallen in love with eighteen years ago, and that woman was right here, gazing at her like she wanted her just as much. Kyla wished she could trust her own eyes. Her own heart. A noisy sob escaped before she could suppress it.

Echo instantly climbed onto their bed, wrapping her arms around Kyla and holding her close. "What's wrong? Please talk to me."

Kyla sobbed, frustrated. "You have no idea what this is like. I need to remember and I keep thinking I'm going to. It's like it's right there, but the more I try to seize on to it, the more it eludes me."

Echo kissed the top of her head and gently rocked her back and forth. She continued to deposit kisses and hold her tight until there were no more sobs. "You doing okay, baby?"

When Echo heard steady breathing in response, she stretched out and eased Kyla to a lying position. As quietly as she could, she disengaged herself, scooped up all the pictures, and put them back in the trunk. She lay back down and watched Kyla sleep, wondering if Kyla knew more than she admitted. Perhaps she could remember tiny fragments but simply hadn't pieced them together yet. Her suspicions made Echo deeply uneasy. Maybe the cops were responsible for making her lose trust. Their blundering around in the mess of Jenny Vasquez hadn't helped. Echo wished she'd never gone to Jenny's place. Even as she'd knocked on the door, she'd known she was making a big mistake. But she was furious with Jenny and wanted to warn her to back off.

Echo got undressed and took a shower to calm the frazzled nerves she kept hidden from Kyla. She wished she knew how to handle the situation. She knew the detectives were trying to rattle her, but they were out of their minds if they thought she was going to tell them what they wanted to hear. She dried off and returned to the bedroom, feeling more relaxed. Cautiously she rolled onto her side and snuggled up to her partner. Until last night's row things had been improving between them and Echo was sure she could win back Kyla's trust. She just needed to be patient, that's all.

❖

Colton was a small child. His hair hung in his eyes as he walked along the familiar path from kindergarten. Kyla sat in the car, waiting to take him to lunch, as was their routine. He liked to feel independent and Kyla let him, but kept her eyes on him at all times.

While she watched, an arm shot from the bushes and grabbed Colton. She could hear him scream and watched him disappear behind the hedge. Kyla was out of her car in a heartbeat, screaming for help, yelling for the man to stop. She ran to the spot where he'd grabbed Colton, but they were gone. She yelled over and over for him. There were people all around picking up their kids. Why didn't they answer? Why wouldn't they help her?

She reached out and woke up covered in a sheen of cold sweat.

"Kyla?" Echo touched her shoulder.

Rolling over, Kyla buried her face in her lover's chest and cried. Illogical fear consumed her. She wasn't one to indulge flights of fancy, but she couldn't shake the horrible feeling of seeing Colton taken from her.

Echo patted her back and cooed to her as she cried. "It's okay, baby. It was just a dream."

"But it felt so real," Kyla whispered.

"You want to tell me about it?"

Kyla shook her head. "You'll just think I'm an idiot."

"Oh, lover. How can you say that? I'd never think that."

"I dreamed that Colton was kidnapped."

Echo sat up straighter. "Oh, my God. How horrible."

"It was. He was such a sweet little boy, walking down the trail after kindergarten."

"I remember that. You used to meet him at the same place every time."

"Exactly. And I was in the car, watching him walk along when all of a sudden a hand grabbed him and he disappeared."

"Oh, Kyla," Echo soothed. "What a terrible nightmare."

"No one would help, no matter how much I screamed."

"No wonder you're so upset. You've really had a bad day or two. Just relax now. I've got you and it's gonna be okay."

Kyla rolled away from her partner and stared at the ceiling. "The thing is, I feel like it's all connected."

"What is?"

"The shooting and the dream."

"You think Colton had something to do with the shooting? I think that's a bit far-fetched."

"No. Not Colton. But something about the dream was so real."

Echo propped herself on an elbow. "Maybe it's that case in the news. The boy missing from Medford. You remember, we saw it on TV just before you came up to bed."

"Yes." Kyla's mind had been elsewhere at the time, but she recalled the police talking about a small boy who'd vanished. "I guess that's what set it off."

Her head hurt as she tried to call up the memory lurking just out of view. She sensed that whatever it was, a door would be unlocked and the events of that night would come rushing back to her. Kyla didn't know whether to dread that moment or hope for it. She was afraid of what she might know and how it could change her life.

❖

Chief Wilson of the Bidwell Police Department had called a mandatory briefing. All members of the department were required to be there. Pat and Magnell squirmed in their seats. They weren't on the case of the missing boy, but the chief required everyone's attendance. When the whole department was present, he began.

"All right, all right, quiet down. We're here to talk about the kid that was kidnapped from Medford. Now I know most of you are working other cases, but I want everyone aware of where we are with this and what you can do to help catch the scumbag who took this child. As most of you know from the BOLO, the boy's name is Joey Andrews. He's six years old with straight dark hair and brown eyes. We're passing around this year's school picture. I can guarantee he isn't the laughing smiling little boy in the picture. He's gotta be terrified."

He paused. "Assuming he's even alive after almost three weeks. Now, there's a vehicle people reported seeing around Joey's school for a couple of weeks before he was grabbed. No one has a great description of it, but it's most likely a dark-colored nineteen-ninety-six Chevy Monte Carlo."

He showed a picture of the make and model.

"Okay, now Smythe and Carter are going to take over."

The detectives stood up. One of them spoke. "As you can imagine, there are various agencies involved in trying to find the person who took Joey. Unfortunately, there are no persons of interest and no descriptions. The profiler has indicated we're seeking a male, late thirties to early forties. The older the suspect is, the less likely that the child is still alive. They believe that younger molesters will keep the children around longer to play with, if you will."

"Those guys don't expect to get caught," Magnell murmured to Pat. "A narcissistic psychology is what we're talking about."

Pat accepted this nugget of wisdom with a polite nod. Magnell liked to consider himself a font of wisdom on the mindsets of criminals. She cast a second glance at him, picking up on a seething anger just below the surface. Every now and then, she detected something unspoken and could almost feel the weight of the words. She had no idea what Magnell kept to himself, and she didn't ask. In their line of work, everyone had experienced something too unbearable to discuss.

"Now, while you all haven't been assigned to this case," the officer continued, "we're asking for your help. Please keep your eyes open for Joey. If you make a traffic stop, check the backseat for him. As you patrol, please be on the lookout for anyone acting suspiciously and pay attention to the behavior of any child who fits Joey's description. I'm sorry we can't give you more on the car. Just remember this shape." He pointed to the picture again. "And that it's a dark color. Remember, we're all on the same team, so thank you for your time and your help. Let's get this guy."

❖

"Is that the check for your car?" Echo asked.

Kyla turned to face her. She looked hard at the blue pools that were Echo's eyes and felt butterflies in her stomach. Try as she might to see guilt or anything negative, all she saw was concern and warmth. "Yeah. They finally reimbursed me."

"So, the weekend will be car shopping, huh?"

"It looks that way."

"I'm almost afraid to ask, but am I going with you?"

Again Kyla was torn. Although all signs pointed to an affair, Echo still adamantly denied it. Kyla had expected her to fold after a couple of days and admit everything. But her denials were so emphatic and she seemed so hurt, Kyla had started to believe her, despite evidence to the contrary.

She'd tried to lose herself in her work, but the thought of her partner's betrayal gnawed at her. She swung back and forth between believing what the detectives had told her and wondering if they'd concocted the whole story. Partners were often the primary suspect in cases like this one, and the police had been known to ignore other evidence because they were swayed by statistical likelihood.

It was still unclear to her, even considering the information about Jenny, why they were so sure Echo was involved in the shooting. Even at her angriest, Kyla had a hard time picturing her peaceful, granola girlfriend shooting anyone, let alone her. And yet the tension between them remained thick. Echo alternated between avoiding her and trying to explain herself. Kyla had continued to sleep in the guest room. Doubts or not, she couldn't bring herself to share a bed with her partner, and she wasn't going to allow Echo to persuade her by using sex as a distraction.

Her stomach was in knots. She was only halfway through the week and had no idea how she'd survive the two remaining days until the weekend. She was hoping to do something with Colton during his days off school, but he'd been so involved in a chemistry project that she hadn't had a chance to ask him.

"What do you think?" Echo asked. "Want me to talk to the salesman?"

Kyla sighed. If she was going to buy a new car, she needed Echo with her. Being well known around town for her business, she could usually talk the price down a little. Car salesmen wanted her to refer any gym clientele in the market for a new ride.

"Sure. We'll go first thing Saturday morning," she said. "Why wait?"

❖

Echo pulled the Escalade into the Chrysler dealership. Kyla had been adamant that she wanted another 300C sedan. Her argument was valid. She'd been in a horrific accident and walked away with little long-term impact.

"Do you know what color you want?"

"I think I'd like another silver one."

The salesman walked out of the office and Echo groaned. "My name's Bruce Payne. What can I show you two today?"

Before Echo could say anything, Kyla answered, "We

don't have any questions right now. I've had a Three Hundred before so I know what I'm looking for."

"Why'd you get rid of it?"

The answer stuck in Kyla's throat.

"Why don't you just give us some time?" Echo asked, steering Kyla away from him. "Are you sure you're up for this?"

"I need my own car. Every time I see the rental, I'm reminded of what happened. I need to move on."

They stood in front of the section of 300s, Kyla grateful for Echo's strong arm around her. She could feel her stomach churn and her heart race. Telling herself she was overreacting, she took a deep breath and stepped toward a silver model. Bruce appeared out of nowhere, reaching around her to unlock the door.

"You've got excellent taste," he said as she stared at the seat. "This baby is top of the line. Why don't you climb in?"

As soon as she settled behind the wheel, Kyla was flooded with flashbacks. She saw herself rolling down her window, calling to someone. She saw a flash and heard a gunshot. Startled, she got out of the car and backed away. She felt searing pain in her head as her legs went limp and she collapsed, crumpling to the ground.

"Don't just stand there," Echo snapped as Bruce looked on in dismay. "Go get her some water or something."

"Is she okay?" he asked, looming over Kyla.

"Just get the water." Echo lifted Kyla's head into her lap and whispered, "Kyla? Baby? You okay? What happened?"

Clinging to the strong, sinewy form of her partner, Kyla let the tears flow. She sobbed until she had nothing left. Suspicions and worries about Echo were forgotten for the moment while she buried her face in Echo's chest and relished the feel of the strong hands caressing her back. She finally drew a deep breath so she could speak.

"It was like I was reliving it. I saw the gun and felt the bullet hit me. It was horrible."

"Did you see who shot you?" Echo asked, her face pale. "Is there anything at all? A face? The clothes? Anything?"

Kyla shook her head, too emotionally drained to contemplate the reasons for Echo's panicky words. "I know one thing, though."

"What's that?"

Kyla laughed weakly. "I'm not buying another Chrysler."

"No," Echo said. "No, I don't imagine you are."

CHAPTER ELEVEN

"J ust got back from the tech department," Pat told Magnell as she walked up carrying Jenny Vasquez's laptop.

Her partner sat up straighter. "No kidding? How many phone calls did it take? This better be worth the wait."

"It wasn't," Pat said, dropping into her chair. "A couple e-mails to and from Flannery, both of a professional nature."

"Nothing personal? *Nada*?"

"I hate to disappoint you, but I don't think there was anything going on between them. Jenny seemed to be flirting in a few e-mails, but Flannery never responded to those."

Magnell raised an eyebrow, no doubt at the use of Jenny's first name, but he kept his censure to himself. "Okay, so she didn't respond by e-mail. Makes sense."

"What do you mean?"

"I see it this way. Vasquez sends an e-mail saying she wants to see Flannery. Flannery gets the e-mail, and rather than hit Reply and leave a paper trail for the girlfriend to find if she ever starts snooping around, she calls Vasquez and says she's on her way."

Pat stared intently at the man across from her before answering. "I think that's a stretch. The e-mails from Flannery were all work related. I mean, there was nothing even remotely suggestive. Nothing to read between the lines. The personal stuff was the bare minimum. 'Hope you enjoyed the Pilates session…Good luck with Mrs. Olberman.' Seriously, based on what's *not* there, it's almost certain there was no affair."

"You're saying Vasquez made it all up?" Magnell threw up his hands in disgust. "Giving a false statement is no laughing matter. Why the blazes would she do that?"

"Maybe she wanted to make trouble for Flannery." Pat couldn't think of any other reason that made sense. "Obviously she had a crush and started rumors at work because she wanted people to think Flannery returned her feelings. Think about it. If she was the boss's secret girlfriend, she could probably wield some power. Then she gets the sack and she's angry and humiliated."

"The woman scorned, huh?"

"Exactly."

"What about threatening e-mails? Did she send anything like that to Flannery?"

Pat shook her head. "No. It looks like the job was over and that was the end of their communication."

"Something's not adding up," Magnell said. "You saw Flannery coming out of that apartment in some kind of state. What was that about if it wasn't…you know…*it*?"

"I think we should ask her," Pat said. "I can take the laptop back and see what she has to say."

Magnell stood. "I'll go with you."

"Actually, Tom, I'd like to see if I can get her to open up. Woman to woman, you know?"

Magnell nodded. "Good plan. Act sympathetic. See if she'll cry on your shoulder."

"I'll work on it," Pat said.

As she left the office she pictured Jenny Vasquez pouring

out a sob story about the affair she'd wished she had with Echo Flannery. Pat wasn't in the mood to offer consolation. She had a much better idea, one that disturbed her equanimity so much she got out of the elevator on the wrong floor. Irritated, she took the stairs the rest of the way. She'd always had a weakness for sexy bad girls whose lives were train wrecks, perhaps because she was the complete opposite. And perhaps she was extra vulnerable right now because today was Valentine's Day and who wanted to be reminded that they had no one to give a card to?

She strolled to her car, trying not to think about the boring state of her love life. She wasn't sure what the attraction was to Jenny, but she was determined to resist it. Desperation wasn't a good enough reason to risk disciplinary action.

❖

Jenny Vasquez opened her door and smiled broadly. "Welcome back. What can I do for you?"

Pat held out her computer. "Actually, I'm just here to return your laptop."

Jenny held her gaze. "Did you find what you were looking for?"

"Well, to be honest, we didn't find anything that indicated an affair between you and Ms. Flannery."

"I told you I didn't think you would. Most of our communicating was done face-to-face. Now, won't you come in?"

Pat stepped into the apartment and once again looked around. It was habit when she was involved in an investigation. As she'd noted on her previous visits, nothing in the apartment seemed out of place or suspicious.

"Please sit down," Jenny said. "Can I get you something to drink?"

Gut instinct warred with basic attraction. Pat knew she should leave, but she couldn't make herself decline the offer. She wanted a drink so she'd have an excuse to stay awhile. The fact that nothing incriminating was found on the computer helped her rationalize her decision. She should try to get a closer look around the apartment. If they could cross Jenny off the list of suspects, they could start focusing on other lines of inquiry. And if Jenny was no longer of interest, what harm could there be in getting to know the attractive woman a little better?

She sat on the couch and said, "A glass of water would be great, if it's no trouble."

Jenny brought her water and sat facing her, one leg tucked under the other and her arm along the back of the couch, inches from Pat's shoulders. Pat instinctively tensed, which brought a reprimand from her hostess. "You need to relax, *querida*. You are safe here."

Her actions contradicted her words as she began to rub Pat's shoulders. Her hands felt incredibly good, her firm caresses soothing and sensual.

"So, did you really have an affair with Flannery?" Pat asked, to distract herself.

"Please, all you ever want to talk to me about is Echo and the affair. There's so much more to me than that. Let's talk about something else."

Pat felt her guard lowering and warned herself to be careful. Still, she relaxed under Jenny's ministrations. "So there's more to you than just being Echo Flannery's mistress, huh? Tell me about yourself."

"What do you want to know?"

"I want to know what you see in Echo Flannery."

Jenny playfully swatted her. "No more Flannery talk. Please."

Pat leaned her head back and closed her eyes. "Okay. How did you end up working at the gym?"

"I was working as a fashion correspondent for KPTV and was unceremoniously replaced by a younger model. I still worked out every day and looked great, so I decided to earn a living helping other women get in shape."

"That's why you look so familiar." Pat studied the striking face just above hers. Jenny was sitting practically on top of her. Pat could smell her scent, a warm, spicy fragrance she recalled from the last time she was here. "I must have seen you on TV. So, why Echo's Cardio?"

Jenny stopped rubbing. "You mean why Echo, don't you? I told you, no more about that. Next subject."

Pat looked into Jenny's normally warm eyes and saw cold flint staring back at her. "I'm sorry, I told you I don't relax when I'm on duty. I can't seem to change the subject because I need some answers. You made a false statement to us, Jenny. I could arrest you for that."

Jenny stroked her arm. "You're not going to arrest me. Can't we just talk for a bit? It's nice to visit."

Pat couldn't look away from the exotic woman. Against her better judgment, she ran her hand along Jenny's arm. Her skin was tantalizingly soft. Pat instantly knew she'd made a mistake. She started to stand, but Jenny pulled her back down.

"What's your hurry, Detective? You are an attractive woman. I am an attractive woman. It's only natural that we would want to get to know each other better. Surely you have more interesting questions for me? I know I have some for you."

Temptation tore at Pat. Jenny intrigued her, pulling her in

like a dangerous narcotic. Still, she forced herself to stand. "I need to get going if you're not planning to cooperate with our inquiries."

Jenny looked up at her, brown eyes solemn. She took a deep breath and exhaled slowly. "There was no affair," she said quietly.

Pat sat back down. "What?"

"There was no affair. I wasn't sleeping with Echo. So you don't need to ask me any more questions about it."

Relief flooded over Pat. If this was true, then Jenny had no motive for trying to kill Kyla. Suspicion quickly moved in. What reason did she truly have to believe this new account? "I'm going to need some verification of that, since you've changed your story. Can you explain why you spread rumors that weren't true?"

"What does it matter now? I told you, I didn't do it."

"And I believe you, so what could have possessed you to lie to the people who work with Echo?"

Jenny ran her hands through her long hair before she answered. "*Querida*, please try to understand. I was good as a fashion correspondent. Damned good. But I passed thirty and my airtime began to dwindle. By the time I turned thirty-two, I was out of a job for being too old. Then I got the job working for Echo and the gym was expanding. We were very busy, working long hours together."

"You developed an infatuation," Pat concluded.

"I suppose you could say that. We had so many long meetings and I admit, I flirted with her. I was lonely."

"You knew she had a partner."

Jenny shrugged. "A partner who made her unhappy."

"Did Echo say that?"

"No, she never talked about her relationship, but it was obvious."

Pat mentally filed that observation away. If Jenny wasn't the cause of conflict in the Flannery-Edmonds home, what was? "Did she flirt with you?"

"Sometimes. All in fun, of course, but some of the other employees noticed there was chemistry." Jenny paused. "Detective, I'd just been fired for being too old. It was good for my ego to have people think I might have captured the attention of Echo Flannery."

"Surely Echo tried to quiet the hype."

"Not really. I think she thought it was harmless."

"Did you ever talk to her about it?"

"What was I going to say? 'Hi, boss. Everyone thinks we're sleeping together. I think we should. What do you say?'"

"Okay." Pat reminded herself that women like Jenny didn't consider home-wrecking a reason to feel bad. What did it matter that Echo had a wife and son, when Jenny's ego needed to be fed? "So the rumors kept going. And you really didn't care. What happened then?"

"I figured if they weren't going to listen to my denials, I'd have a little fun. You know, mess with their heads. You need to remember that Echo is gorgeous. I wasn't the only one who flirted with her."

Pat could imagine, with a gym full of female clients, there were probably more than a few who would see Echo as fair game. "And how did you mess with their heads?"

"You know." Jenny shrugged. "I did little things to feed the fire. I made sure to spend extra time in Echo's office whenever I could. I also made it a point to be out of the gym whenever she was. It was pretty funny. Before I knew it, everyone was sure we were sleeping together. I whipped them into a frenzy."

"And you didn't correct that impression?"

A flash of embarrassment darted across Jenny's level stare and momentarily contracted her features. Pat was relieved to glimpse, even briefly, this evidence of a conscience. "This is a lot to digest, Jenny."

"But it also shows I'm innocent. I didn't kill anyone. That is good for us, yes?"

Pat studied Jenny's face, wanting to believe she meant no harm and had simply acted thoughtlessly when she was at a low point. Seeing an unexpected softness in her eyes when she smiled, she kissed the hot Latina's cheek and said, "I'll give it some serious thought."

Jenny walked her to the door. Holding it open, she said, "I'll be waiting."

Chapter Twelve

Kyla sat at her desk, focusing on tax forms she was preparing when her receptionist walked into her office carrying a large floral arrangement. She set the arrangement of red roses, white carnations, baby's breath, and fern on the credenza and handed the card to Kyla before she left.

With a strange sense of detachment, Kyla read: *Kyla, we've been through a rough patch, but I still love you. Tell me you'll still be my Valentine?* She threw the card on her desk and rested her head on her hands. The last thing she wanted to do was think about her relationship with Echo. Tax season was underway and she planned to bury herself in her work. She hadn't even considered that it was Valentine's Day.

She picked up the card and read it again. How could Echo say she still loved her? Did she really expect Kyla to believe that? Kyla couldn't seem to get herself to trust Echo. She desired her; actually, she hadn't felt so sexually aware of her in years. Yet she was no longer sure if she loved her. She wondered if she would ever be able to feel comfortable around her again, let alone experience the complete oneness they'd once shared.

The phone rang, startling her from her reverie. "How's your day going?" The familiar voice sparked a slight leap in

Kyla's pulse. It did that, these days, no matter how uncertain she felt.

"The flowers are nice, Echo."

"Oh, good. I'm glad you like them."

There was an uneasy silence.

"Kyla…"

"No, Echo. No. Look, the flowers were a nice gesture. But I'm not ready to agree to happily ever after. I can't just go back to the way everything was. There are too many questions. I don't know how I feel anymore. So I can't promise to be your Valentine to have and to hold from this day forward. I just can't do it."

"What about dinner?" Echo asked softly.

Kyla was bewildered. It was as if Echo wasn't listening to anything she said. "Dinner?"

"Yes. Can I take you to dinner tonight?"

"I don't know if that's such a good idea."

"Why? We have dinner together at home all the time. It's the same thing, only at a restaurant."

Kyla latched on to an excuse. "What about Colton?"

"He's not five anymore. He'll be fine. He can fend for himself for once."

"Still…it seems awfully intimate."

"I'm asking for dinner, Ky. Not sex. Just dinner. Just agree to dinner."

Kyla was in no mood to argue. She sighed. "Fine. We'll go to dinner tonight. Now, will you let me get back to work, please?"

"Sure. I'll see you when you get home."

❖

Echo pulled the Escalade into the restaurant parking lot while Kyla sat sullenly in the passenger seat. As she parked, Echo asked, "Are you going to be like this all night?"

"I don't really have a lot to say to you, Echo. I knew this wasn't a good idea."

"I disagree. We need this. You need it. I need it. We need it."

They walked inside in strained silence. The hostess led them past table after table of happy couples holding hands and whispering suggestively to each other. Kyla was sure she and Echo would never again share the level of comfort those other couples did. She chided herself for ever agreeing to the date. Why was she trying to please Echo? Her partner had lost interest in her a long time ago, even if she was going through the motions now. That thought filled Kyla with grim suspicions. Why would Echo bother?

Once seated, Kyla hid behind her menu, attempting to completely block out the distracting sight of her partner. Echo looked good in her plain navy cotton shirt and tailored linen slacks. She turned heads as she walked through the restaurant. Echo always claimed that her height attracted attention. Kyla thought it was her walk, graceful but powerful, showing off the physique of a woman who enjoyed her body and made it work. Every time she saw that body, clothed or not, she found herself staring as if she'd never seen it before. As if she hadn't slept with Echo for the past eighteen years. She didn't know what to make of her sudden fascination for her partner. Her memory loss must have caused it. She felt displaced in so many ways, perhaps it wasn't surprising that her partner felt less familiar to her.

She stared sightlessly at her menu. She wasn't even hungry. She felt restless and upset and wished she hadn't agreed to this farce. Valentine's Day. What did it mean? A celebration of enduring love or an excuse to feign deep emotion one day a year?

She jumped slightly as a hand tugged her menu down and Echo looked her in the eye. "Do you think we can try to communicate?"

"I was just looking at my menu. We can communicate after we order, can't we?"

"I suppose. Unless you come up with some other way to avoid me."

Kyla didn't answer as she lifted her menu again as a shield. After they'd ordered, she leaned back in her seat and looked around the restaurant, determined to look everywhere but at her partner.

"What's it going to take?" Echo asked.

"What do you mean?"

"What will it take to get you to relax around me? Why won't you trust me?"

"How can I trust you? You keep secrets from me. You sneak around. You have an affair. What else? How can I not keep wondering what else you haven't told me?"

"Kyla, I've never had an affair. Please, it's Valentine's Day. Let's try to make a new start."

Kyla sighed and remained silent. Echo stared at her, but she refused to make eye contact. The lack of conversation dragged on, punctuated with periodic attempts by Echo to start a discussion. Kyla gave polite answers but refused to be drawn along the track Echo wanted to take her. She didn't want to hear any more justifications.

Their dinners finally arrived, giving them something to do. They ate in stilted silence until Echo slammed her fork down. "This is ridiculous. Look, you agreed to this date. Say something, for Christ's sake."

"My steak is really good," Kyla responded.

Echo laughed. "Well, that's a start."

Kyla looked up. "How's your salmon?"

"It's good, too." Their gazes met.

"I have something to tell you," Echo said.

Kyla cut another slice of steak. "I'm listening."

"I know you suspect me of something. An affair, or worse. And I know you only think that way because you can't trust yourself. You can't remember important things, so you're filling in the gaps."

Kyla didn't raise her voice, but she spoke icily. "I can't believe you're making this my fault."

A spark of anger lit Echo's eyes, mixing with another emotion that made Kyla's stomach hollow. Echo concentrated on her face as though drinking her in. "I've been a fool." Her eyes welled and emotion thickened her words. "You've been right in front of me all these years, and at some point I stopped seeing you. I...stepped back."

Kyla felt the air rush from her lungs. She lowered her fork, unable to take another bite. Echo's expression was so naked, she couldn't tear her gaze away. She wasn't sure when she'd last seen that look.

"Listen to me," Echo said. "And stop listening to those other voices. Those doubts. I almost lost you a month ago and if that had happened I think I would have died. I know I haven't handled everything perfectly since the accident. But it makes me crazy to think someone tried to take you away from me." Her voice fractured and she reached for Kyla's hand. "I'm asking you, for the sake of all the years we've spent together, to trust me. I love you. I've always loved you."

Kyla's mouth trembled. If Echo was lying, she was quite an actress—and Kyla had never known her to be a phony. She stared down at the hand firmly clasping hers. She could feel a warm current from those fingers and sense the deep emotion in her partner. Wanting to give room to the chance of that new start Echo was asking for, she said, "I wish things were like they used to be."

"Me, too." Echo sighed. "There's a lot we haven't said to each other for a while. Sometimes I haven't been completely open with you because I didn't want to hurt you."

Kyla swallowed a lump of pain. Finally, the admission she'd been waiting for. "I think it's best just to get it out in the open. Secrets make themselves felt."

"I know." Echo's fingers tightened. "There are things you haven't told me, too."

"Like what?" Kyla couldn't think of anything she'd kept from Echo. She'd always leaned on her strength and sought her opinions. She'd always told her everything.

A trace of sadness filtered into Echo's faint smile. "I'm not going to spend tonight rehashing the past. I want us to look to the future."

"Too much has happened for us just to move on as if it's not important."

"I disagree, baby," Echo said patiently. "Everything that we've been through should bring us closer together, not split us apart. After almost losing you, I'm not willing to live in a stalemate because of issues that just don't matter anymore."

"I don't know how you can be so dismissive," Kyla said. "Under normal circumstances, what I've been through should have brought us closer." She decided to be open about her biggest reservation. "But I feel like there's something important you're not telling me and it makes me feel stuck."

Echo lifted Kyla's hand to her mouth and gently kissed it. "I keep telling you I've done nothing wrong. You need to relax and trust me. I feel like we keep taking one step forward and two back."

"That's because whenever I finally feel like I can trust

you, like tonight, I learn another secret. Honestly, Echo. Don't make yourself out to be some sort of martyr."

Echo paid the check. "We've had a nice evening. Let's not ruin it." She patted her stomach. "We survived."

"That we did. And it was nice. Thank you."

"My pleasure, my lady." As they walked to the car, Echo said, "Whatever happens, whether you get your memory back or not, I want to make a promise to you."

They stopped walking and stood in the crisp winter air. Echo wrapped her arms around Kyla and braced her, to take the weight of her crutches. Cupping a hand to Kyla's cheek, she kissed her sweetly on the lips and said, "I promise you will never have a reason to distrust me. I will always keep you safe and if anyone tries to hurt you...I'll kill them."

Kyla looked into her eyes and felt a terrible guilt. How could she have suspected Echo for a moment? Her partner of eighteen years was gazing at her with such sincerity, she had to accept her words at face value.

"I believe you," she said, as a burst of optimism shook the doubt from her soul. All of a sudden she felt sure she'd made a dreadful mistake pushing Echo away. Echo's lips brushed hers and Kyla responded by inviting her in. Shivering with cold and yearning, she whispered, "Take me home."

Echo kissed her deeply and hungrily, as though she couldn't bear for their mouths to move apart again. "Will you sleep with me?" she asked between one stroke of her tongue and the next.

"Yes," Kyla said, swaying in closer, loving the feel of Echo's strong arms and solid torso. "I love you."

"Oh, baby." Echo smiled her unforgettable smile. "I love you, too."

❖

Pat stepped out of her Nissan Frontier pickup and, taking a deep breath, smoothed out imagined wrinkles from her black silk shirt and jeans. She still wasn't sure what had possessed her to call Jenny Vasquez and ask her out. Their last intense conversation had left so much unanswered, Pat wasn't sure she even wanted to talk again. Or if she was interested in the answers, anyway. But she was deeply curious about Jenny and wasn't sure she could go on pretending she wasn't. For the moment, all she cared about was that there hadn't been an affair between Echo Flannery and Jenny, so the gorgeous Latina was no longer off-limits.

She waited anxiously for Jenny to answer her knock. It seemed like hours before the door was finally opened. The view was worth the wait. Jenny was dressed in a skintight zebra-striped dress that barely reached her thighs. The top of her dress was cut low, showing off her ample breasts, the short sleeves accenting her toned upper arms.

Pat had to force herself to stop staring. "You look very nice," she managed.

"Thank you. Come in."

Pat handed her a dozen orange roses.

"Orange?"

"Red seemed a bit forward."

"I like forward." Jenny leaned in and brushed Pat's lips.

"I'm sure you do." Pat took a step back. "We should probably get going. Our reservations are in fifteen minutes."

"Sit. We'll have a drink first."

Pat wiped her palms on her jeans. She was nervous. "I really don't want to be late."

"You worry too much." Jenny playfully pushed her onto the couch, making sure to dangle her breasts over her.

Taking a deep breath, Pat slid out from under the tempting

body. "I just don't want to lose a table. Now, do you have a coat or something?"

"Do you think I need to be covered up?"

"I just thought…there's a chill in the air."

"I'm sure you'll keep me warm," Jenny whispered.

Pat chastised herself. She wanted to be strong, but her body was responding to Jenny, making it hard to concentrate. "Okay then. Let's get going."

She held the door open and Jenny slipped past her, brushing against her as she did. They made small talk on the drive to the restaurant, but once in the red leather booth across from each other, they fell into an uncomfortable silence. Pat was relieved when they could place their orders. At least the waitress was someone to talk to. After she left, Pat stared at Jenny's almond-shaped eyes, losing herself in the warm chocolate.

Jenny stared back, licking her dark red lips and beckoning to Pat with her gaze. Pat searched her mind for something to say. Finally she decided to try to get Jenny to talk about herself. "So, were you born and raised in the Portland area?"

"No. What about you?"

"Bidwell, born and bred. Where are you from, then?"

Jenny looked bored. "Northern California. Why do people make such a big deal out of where someone is from anyway?"

Pat shrugged. "I just want to get to know you better."

"Then let's skip dinner and go back to my place."

Pat's heart raced. The idea of taking Jenny home and making love to her instantly aroused her. She fought to maintain control, determined to know more about Jenny than her name and a brief recent employment history. "What brought you to Portland?"

"School. I went to University of Portland to study communications."

Pat stared hard at the mysterious woman across from her. Normally an excellent judge of character, she was perplexed by Jenny's statement. UoP was a private university and Jenny didn't strike her as having come from money. Neither did she seem the type to work to put herself through college.

"Why are you looking at me like that?" Jenny accused. "You don't think I could get into a school like that?"

"I don't doubt that you could get into it. You're a very intelligent lady. I just know that it costs a pretty penny to go there."

Jenny shrugged, fueling Pat's curiosity. "You want to explain that shrug?" she asked.

"I don't want to talk about things from so long ago. Surely we can find something better to discuss." Jenny smiled. "Like how that shirt makes your eyes sparkle."

"Have I told you how beautiful you look tonight?"

"You have not."

Pat grinned, knowing that she had. "Well, you do. That dress is absolutely stunning."

"Just the dress, huh?"

"No, not just the dress."

Jenny's smile broadened. "Thank you."

The mutual admiration was interrupted when the waitress brought their meals. As soon as she walked off, Jenny started again. She leaned forward, showing her cleavage before asking, "So, what do you like best about my dress?"

Pat swallowed hard and wiped her palms again. "I like how form fitting it is."

Jenny licked her lips and winked. "Maybe tonight you can peel it off and see the form underneath."

"That's a very interesting fantasy."

"Why stop there? I believe in exploring fantasies, don't you?"

"It depends." Pat turned her attention to her meal before her face went completely red. Heat glowed in her cheeks and her mouth felt dry. She was so easy, succumbing to Jenny's well-practiced flirtation routine without even token resistance. As they ate, she attempted to get more information on Jenny's past. "So where in California did you say you were from?"

"Northern."

"Northern like San Francisco?"

"Further north. Why don't you tell me about your childhood?"

"Mine?" Pat was surprised. Most of her dates were happy to talk about themselves all evening. "Well, my father was a cop in the Bidwell PD and I pretty much grew up with the stigma of being a cop's daughter."

Jenny snorted.

"What? You don't think people make fun of cops' kids? Especially in small towns like Bidwell?"

"That kind of prejudice is nothing."

"I don't think I used that word."

"You implied it. Life's so rough for the daughter of a cop. That's why you went on to become one. You wouldn't know rough."

"Oh no? Then tell me, what did your daddy do?"

"He worked in agriculture."

Pat was surprised. She had detected more of an accent than she usually heard in Jenny's voice. "Yeah? In what capacity?"

Jenny moved a piece of steak around on her plate, then let out a heavy sigh. "If you must know, he was a farm worker."

Hence the accent, Pat thought. More intrigued than ever, she proceeded with caution. "That can be a brutal job. What kind of crop did he work with?"

Jenny shrugged. "Whatever crop was in season."

Pat stared at her date as she sipped her water, trying to make it all fit. Jenny did not seem to belong in a migrant farm worker mold. "Okay, so growing up as a migrant farmer's kid was probably rougher than as a cop's. Did you ever work in the fields?"

"Do I look like I worked in a field?"

"No." Pat laughed. "Actually, you don't. So how does someone from farms in northern California end up as a fashion correspondent in Portland?"

"It was what I wanted. I'm used to getting what I want."

Pat was saved from having to respond by the waitress appearing to clear the table and leaving the bill. Once they'd paid, they walked out to the truck in silence.

"Thank you for dinner," Jenny said as she strapped herself in.

"Thank you. I really enjoyed myself. You're a fascinating woman, Jenny Vasquez." As they drove off, she asked, "So how is it that you always get what you want?"

"I learned at a very young age how to work people."

"How so?"

"People like attractive people. They like to think attractive people like them. I was a cute kid. I learned that if I was friendly to people who could help me, they would."

"Just how friendly were you?"

She shrugged. "Not like that. Men are easy to use. And I didn't do anything with them. I've known I was a lesbian since I was very young. But I was always sure to hang out with people who had something I needed."

"You networked," Pat said. It was kinder than thinking of Jenny as a user.

"You could say that." Jenny's smile was cynical. "Tutors to help me with my grades. Cheerleaders to help me make the squad. People who could help me be more normal and less poor Mexican. That's how I got my full-ride scholarship to UoP."

"So, should I be nervous?" Pat asked. "Am I being worked?"

"I wouldn't say you're being worked, but I definitely want you. And—"

"You always get what you want."

"Would you like to come in?" Jenny asked as Pat parked the truck.

"I'd love to."

Jenny held out her hand and Pat took it, its softness causing her heart to jump. She cautioned herself not to get carried away. She could ill afford to compromise her career over a soft, voluptuous woman with teasing eyes and full red lips. When Jenny let them into her apartment and turned to her, Pat's resolve wavered. She cupped Jenny's jaw and stroked it lightly as she pulled her close, her lips barely brushing Jenny's. Jenny's arms slid around her neck, pressing her closer. The kiss intensified. Jenny's mouth opened slightly, inviting Pat's tongue in. Slowly, tentatively, she slid her tongue against Jenny's lips, tracing them, memorizing them.

Jenny's tongue moved more forcefully, dancing around Pat's and exploring every inch of the warm, moist area until they were hungrily sampling one another, moaning and grinding, barely pausing to catch their breath.

Pat pulled Jenny closer, frustrated by the clothes that stood between them. Jenny walked them to the couch and lay down, pulling Pat on top of her. Pat frantically kissed her, bringing her knee up between Jenny's legs. When she felt Jenny's fingers unbuttoning her shirt, she suddenly came to her senses.

"Whoa," she said, pushing herself up and off.

Jenny wrapped a leg around her, preventing her escape. "What are you doing?"

Pat slid out and stood on shaky legs. "I can't do this. It's not right."

"It sure felt right to me."

"Not yet," Pat said emphatically. "Not until everything is straightened out."

"I thought everything *was* straightened out."

"Not officially. And something like this could cost me my career."

Jenny frowned. "How can you think of your career at a time like this?"

"How can I not?" Pat buttoned her shirt and walked to the door. "I'll call you."

Once in her truck, she rested her forehead on her steering wheel, appalled at how close she'd come to losing control. She took a deep breath and turned the key in the ignition. She glanced up and could see Jenny standing in the front window of her apartment, backlit by the soft lamplight in her living room. For a few seconds, Pat was dangerously close to going right back up there and tearing off Jenny's clothes. But she forced herself to drive away, filled with even greater resolve to find out who shot the Edmonds woman and prove Jenny innocent once and for all.

CHAPTER THIRTEEN

Kyla let herself into her sister-in-law Sierra's house fully prepared for a high school drama. Colton had called a half hour earlier, asking to be picked up and refusing to walk home.

"So what's the big deal?" she asked him.

"Why don't you sit down?" Sierra said.

Dread crept into Kyla's stomach. "What happened? What's going on?"

"The boys had kind of a creepy incident walking home from school this afternoon."

Kyla looked to Colton. "Define creepy."

"Some weirdo was checking us out."

"Apparently a man in a dark car was driving along watching the boys," Sierra explained.

"Not both of us," Levi offered. "The dude didn't take his eyes off Colton."

Panic began to set in for Kyla. "Who was this guy? Have you ever seen him before?"

"Never," Colton said. "It was way scary. And he followed us all the way up Monroe Drive. So we walked past our block and I came home with Levi."

Kyla reached for her purse and fumbled through it for a business card. She grabbed her cell phone and started dialing.

"Silverton," a disembodied voice answered at the other end.

"This is Kyla Edmonds."

"Ms. Edmonds. What can I do for you?"

"I'm at Echo's sister's house. I need you to come up here so my son can tell you what happened to him this afternoon." She gave the address, hung up, and began to pace as best she could, with her plaster cast clunking on the floor.

"Mom, chill."

"Really, Kyla. It was probably nothing." Sierra tried to calm her.

"How do we know? How can we be sure it wasn't related?"

"Related to what?" Sierra's small oval face grew pinched. "You mean the…accident? Why would there be any connection?"

"I don't know. But it feels like there is. I can't explain it."

"They're two unrelated events," Sierra said in a soothing tone.

"No." Kyla shook her head adamantly. "It's too coincidental."

"With the station just down on the corner of Monroe and Oasis, it'll only take the police a few minutes to get here," Sierra said. "So you'd better come up with something more to tell them."

"Why are you acting like I'm crazy? Don't you believe in just feeling things sometimes?" Kyla's pacing was interrupted by a knock on the door.

Sierra raced to let the detectives in. She brought them to the kitchen where the two teenagers stood looking mortified.

As Kyla performed the introductions, the boys shook hands with the detectives.

"Someone want to tell us what's going on here?" Magnell asked.

"It wasn't that big of a deal," Colton said. "Some car followed us home today."

"It was more than that," Levi said. "The guy drove really slow and never took his eyes off Colton, I swear."

"What did this guy look like?" Pat Silverton asked.

"He was old," Colton said. "And he had big ol' sunglasses on and a baseball cap."

Taking down notes, Silverton asked, "How old?"

Colton looked toward Magnell. "Not as old as him."

Kyla and Sierra quickly turned away to hide their smiles.

"So more like your mom's age?" Silverton asked.

"I guess."

"What about the car?"

"It was dark gray," Levi said. "And old. Like nineties."

"Two doors or four?"

The boys looked at each other before Colton answered. "Four."

"Yeah, four." Levi agreed. "I noticed his license plate had FCM on it."

Magnell raised an eyebrow. "Why would you notice that?"

Colton blushed bright red. "He thought it stood for Fuckin' Child Molester."

Kyla stared in disbelief at her son.

"It made sense," Colton mumbled. "You had to be there."

"Okay," Silverton said. "Did you notice anything else about the car?"

Colton shook his head. "There wasn't like a logo or

anything, you know? So I don't know what kind it was. The plates were the basic tree plates. That's all I remember."

"You said he never looked away from you? Seems like he would have had a hard time driving like that." Magnell sounded like he had the bullshit meter running, and, so far, the story registered right up there with life on Mars.

"Yeah, until we got to Levi's street. Then he just smiled at me and kept driving."

"Well, thanks for the information. We'll look into this." Magnell heaved himself off a bar stool.

"So, what do you think?" Kyla asked anxiously.

"What do *I* think?" Magnell repeated. "I think some perv from Portland is cruising the suburbs, trolling for pretty boys."

"I'm not a pretty boy." Colton looked offended.

"I didn't mean to imply you were. But the eyes of a molester see things differently."

Kyla stroked Colton's hair. Her son seemed to be growing up too fast. At fourteen, he still had some boyishness left to his looks, but his jaw was becoming more square and his voice was starting to change. There was peach fuzz on the tip of his chin and more definition to his body. She loved that he was young enough not to have to worry about dating, although, admittedly, she was looking forward to his outgrowing his two main interests, video games and his guitar. Both involved his cousin Levi. The two were nearly inseparable. Everyone referred to them as an odd couple, with Colton being tall, thin, pale, and blond, and Levi being of moderate height and weight, with dark hair and complexion.

Kyla was afraid. "Do you think it could be connected?" she pumped the detectives.

"To your shooter?" Silverton wore a dubious expression.

"Yes. Is it possible he found out I'm still alive and that I have a son and now he's going after Colton?"

"That's pretty far-fetched," Magnell said.

"But it's possible."

Magnell opened his mouth, but before he could say anything, Silverton answered. "We have no way of knowing at this point. But I'll tell you what. We'll run the information your son has given us and see if we can get an ID on the guy who drove that car. Then we'll take it from there, okay?"

Kyla nodded, knowing there wasn't much else she could ask for at that point. "Thank you."

"Thanks for calling us. We'll let you know as soon as we find anything."

Out at the car, Magnell immediately chastised Pat. "What were you doing, offering false hope?"

"Who says it's false hope? What if she's right?"

"And what if pigs fly?"

"We both know a lead in any direction would be welcome in her case right now," she reminded him. It had been almost a month since the shooting and, so far, their relentless focus on Echo Flannery had led them to a big fat dead end.

"A lead, yes." Magnell dropped into the passenger seat like he was exhausted. "Preferably a legitimate one."

"This could be legit. We can't determine that until we rule it out."

Magnell shook his head as she started the car. "Sometimes I wonder what in the hell world you live in."

❖

Jenny Vasquez pulled her Miata into a space in the Echo's Cardio parking lot. Unaccustomed to the role she found herself in, she was experiencing nerves for the first time in decades. She knew she was doing the right thing, but that didn't make it easy. She climbed out of the car and pulled her coat tightly around her. She'd worn jeans, not too tight, and a brown turtleneck sweater. She looked good, as usual, but not overly seductive. This had to be done right.

As she opened the front door of the gym, she was immediately aware of the focus on her. She passed the front desk, where Meadow Tenori stood staring in disbelief and no small measure of condemnation.

"I know the way," she said, walking straight past the receptionist and making her way to Echo's office.

Her former boss looked up sharply when she pushed the door open. "What are you doing here?"

"We need to talk." Jenny stepped inside.

"No. We don't." Echo stood. "Good-bye."

"Please, sit down. Please let me talk to you." Jenny moved to close the door behind her.

"Leave it open," Echo said. "Have a seat, if you must." She pointed to a chair in front of her desk. "What reason could you possibly have for being here?"

Jenny stared at Echo's cold blue eyes and thought what an attractive woman she was, even angry. An affair with her would have been even better than Jenny could have imagined. How could anyone really blame her for encouraging those rumors? Still, now that she was there, her stomach began to churn. In completely uncharted territory, she took a deep breath, and said what she'd come to say.

"Echo, I owe you an apology."

"Just one?" Echo sank back in her chair and interlocked her fingers behind her head.

"Well, if it wasn't for encouraging the rumors, a lot of your other problems never would have come to be."

"And if by other problems, you mean troubles with my business and potential loss of my relationship with Kyla, I suppose you're right."

"Your business was never really in trouble." Jenny dismissed the idea with a flippant shrug.

"I had employees quit because they didn't respect me and customers leave because your schedule was so erratic they never knew when you'd be here for classes," Echo said. "Losing workers and clients generally counts as a business problem."

"Okay. I understand. What started out as a way to make fun of busybodies got way out of hand. And you got hurt. I'm truly sorry."

Echo folded her arms and stared at the woman who had become the bane of her existence. "Why, Jenny? Why now?"

Jenny looked into her eyes and hoped her sincerity showed. "Because it's time. This has gone on long enough. We both need to put it behind us and move on."

"So you want me to forgive you for what you called 'a way to make fun of busybodies'? You were having a good laugh while my world crumbled and now you want me to say it's okay?"

Jenny hadn't anticipated that it would be this hard. She'd known she would have to apologize. She could now tell Pat that she'd done that. But did her apology have to be accepted? She hadn't taken that into consideration. She stood up and pleaded with her best puppy-dog eyes. "I'm sorry, Echo. I don't know what else to say. Can we talk about it? I really want to make things right."

Echo shuffled some papers absently. "Are you turning over a new leaf? It's hard to believe, I guess."

"I didn't expect this, either."

"Did it ever occur to you to think about the consequences

of being a home-wrecker?" Echo asked. "We have a son. He's never done a thing to harm you, but for your entertainment, you placed his security and happiness at risk. What kind of person does that?"

"The kind a woman like you would never get involved with," Jenny answered honestly.

"I think that's a compliment."

Echo's blue eyes seemed to intensify with her smile, and Jenny was reminded of everything she'd daydreamed about. She'd known Echo wouldn't be won over after a few weeks of trying. She'd looked straight past Jenny's looks and seductive ploys to the woman within and found something lacking. Jenny was starting to feel exactly the same way.

"It's a compliment," she confirmed. "You're a special person, Echo. I'm sorry I lost your friendship and your respect."

Echo met her eyes. "I'm sorry, too. None of us can do this alone, you know. We all need to care."

Jenny smiled. "I think I'm finally realizing that."

❖

"Thanks for everything," Kyla said as Colton helped her into the passenger seat next to Sierra, who had volunteered to drive her into town.

"I'm just glad the boys are okay," Sierra answered. "I'll plan on Colton coming home with Levi for a while until things calm down."

"I appreciate that," Kyla said as they backed out of the driveway. She glanced behind her at her son. "Seriously, sweetheart, how are you doing?"

Colton lifted his left shoulder. "I'm okay. I'll be a lot better if I never see that freako again."

Kyla wanted to give him a hug, but her ribs were too sore for her to strain and reach back. "We won't let him get near you," she assured him.

"I know. Do you really think we had to call the cops?"

"I do."

"Because you were shot?"

"Even if I hadn't been shot, we needed to report that some weirdo followed you home. Next time he might do more than just follow you."

"Oh, *that* helps calm me down," Colton said sarcastically.

"Or he might find another boy. But we'll keep you safe," she assured him again.

"I know." He looked down their street as she drove past it. "Where are we going?"

"I thought we'd go see Echo and tell her what happened. Then she can drive us home."

He rolled his eyes but settled in for the short ride to the gym. When they arrived, Colton held the front door for Kyla, who hobbled awkwardly through the gap. She waved at Meadow, who was working the front desk.

"Hi, you two." Meadow looked very uncomfortable. "What are you doing here?"

"We just need to see Echo for a minute," Kyla called to her.

"Colton, perfect timing." Meadow emerged from behind her desk and grabbed his arm. "I have some questions about a video game. Can you come help me?"

Kyla told him, "Go ahead. This should only take a minute."

Again, she noted the odd look on Meadow's face, but her mind was on her son's afternoon. She moved down the hallways as quickly as she could. Echo had someone in her office. She could hear the sound of voices. She stopped mid-stride when she saw Jenny Vasquez standing unnecessarily close to Echo. Kyla cleared her throat and both women looked around.

Echo stepped past Jenny and closed the distance to Kyla. "What's wrong? Why are you here? Is everything okay?"

"No, Echo. Everything is *not* okay." Kyla stared in disbelief at Jenny Vasquez. The woman looked like a porn actress. "You're still carrying on with this strumpet? How dare you."

Jenny walked over to join them. "I am *not* a strumpet. And we are *not* carrying on."

"Well then, what in the hell are you doing here?" Kyla demanded.

"She came to apologize," Echo said.

"Oh sure. And what's she sorry for? Sleeping with you?"

"For saying I did," Jenny said quietly.

"For *what*?" Kyla asked in disbelief.

"You heard her, Ky. She's admitting that there was no affair."

Kyla closed her eyes and willed her head to stop spinning. Echo took her elbow and steered her to a chair, which she gratefully accepted. "I don't understand," Kyla said. "Why are you doing this? Why now?"

"It should have been much sooner." Jenny had the grace to look embarrassed. "I caused you a lot of pain, Kyla. Please believe me when I say I am very, very sorry."

"Sorry? You're *sorry*? That's supposed to make the past year just go away?"

"I know I can't make up for what I've done. But please at least believe that nothing ever happened between Echo and me. Nothing."

Echo squatted in front of Kyla. "Do you hear that? There was no affair."

Kyla got out of her chair and stood toe to toe with Jenny. "I hear your words. I don't know if I believe you or not. And I'm certainly not ready to forgive you. But now you listen to me, Jenny Vasquez. You are not sleeping with my partner and you are not working at this gym. So there is no reason for you to *ever* contact Echo ever again. Do you understand? I never want to hear your name again. Do not call, do not come by. Nothing. Am I making myself clear?"

Jenny looked from one woman to the other.

Echo spoke first. "Kyla—"

"No." Kyla remained focused on Jenny. "I need to hear this from her."

"You have my word," Jenny said.

"For whatever that's worth," Kyla answered. Facing Echo, she said, "Our son is here and he needs us. Get that woman out of my sight and come take us home."

❖

The fireworks had finally died down and Meadow was quite happy not to have Echo, Kyla, or Jenny at the gym anymore. With only a few patrons still there, she was wiping down some of the equipment and getting a head start on her closing duties when the bells on the front door jingled, signaling that someone had walked in. She turned to see a man in his forties approach the desk.

"Hi," she said, returning to her chair. "What can I do for you?"

"I'd like to join your gym," the man said in a nasal tone with the trace of an accent.

Meadow willed herself not to pass judgment. Clients came in all shapes and sizes. This one was average looking, about six feet tall, probably two hundred pounds. His face was full but not fat, and he had a heavy five o'clock shadow. His hair was short, cut above his collar, and he wore a red baseball cap. His eyes were the only thing distinctive about him. They were an eerily light green, almost silvery. Something about his stare made her very uncomfortable.

"You're not from around here, are you?" she asked pleasantly. "How did you hear about our gym?"

He darted quick looks around the interior, but answered calmly. "I've heard really great things about this place. I've heard it's top notch. I can see the equipment is top of the line."

Meadow tried to keep the sarcasm out of her voice. "Well, I'm sorry to tell you, sir, but this gym is for women only."

"Women only?" He looked around again. "I'd think you'd be a lot busier if that's the case."

"You would? And why's that?"

"Didn't a woman get shot in this town recently?"

"How did you hear about that?" Meadow found his attitude strange. And his pale eyes and fleshy hands made her flesh crawl.

"I saw it in the papers." He turned to watch some women on machines.

"I'm sorry, sir, but I'm going to have to ask you to leave. There really are no men allowed."

"Yeah, yeah. I get it. That's my point. How come more women aren't working out? Don't they want to be able to defend themselves?"

Meadow stared hard at him. "What would they have to defend themselves from?"

"Well, whoever shot that woman might go after other

women, right?" He seemed to find this idea amusing and wiped at his wet smile as if it were splashing the surrounding flesh. "Isn't that the way it works? They choose the weak and ignore the strong?"

Meadow shook her head, less at ease with each passing moment. "Our town doesn't have a lot of violence. That was an isolated incident."

"You hope so, right?" He looked around again, then asked, "How's that woman doing, anyway? She better? She didn't die or anything, right?"

"She's fine," Meadow answered hesitantly.

"Good. Her girlfriend or whatever works here, right?"

"You sure ask a lot of questions."

"I just like to know stuff, you know? Is that true? Is she really one of those carpet munchers?"

"Seriously? It's time for you to leave, sir. I've let you stay way too long."

"Yeah, yeah, I'm going. Nice talking to you, though. Can I call you sometime or something?"

"You're not really my type," Meadow said. "Now please go."

She watched the creepy stranger leave but couldn't make out many details of his car through the gym's tinted windows. She could only tell it was a dark-colored four-door older model. She made a mental note to tell Echo about him before their next shift.

CHAPTER FOURTEEN

Kyla woke up Saturday morning to see Echo leaning on the doorjamb of her room, a cup of coffee in each hand. Wondering how Echo could be so damned handsome at such an ungodly hour, she sat up and rubbed her eyes. "What are you doing here?"

"We need to talk."

"For this you stalk me?"

"I'm not stalking you." Echo smiled. "Can I come in?"

"Sure. Sit." Kyla patted the bed next to her and took the coffee she was offered. She was acutely aware that this was the closest Echo had been to being in this bed with her since Valentine's Day. She could feel the heat radiating off her partner but was determined not to let her awareness show. "What's so important that it can't wait until I'm awake?"

Echo sat stiffly on the edge of the bed. She took a deep breath. "We need to talk about a lot of stuff, babe. How about we start with Jenny?"

"Oh, God. I am so tired of hearing that name."

"I'm sure you are, but we can put all that behind us now. I need to know we're on the same page here. You were giving me the cold shoulder last night, and I understand you were angry about seeing her in my office. But I don't want you doing that anymore, okay?"

"And you feel you should spring this on me before I can think clearly?"

Echo laughed. "Hey, I brought coffee."

"I'll give you that." Kyla smiled back, chiding herself for falling prey to Echo's charm so easily.

Echo didn't know it yet, but Kyla was halfway to being in love with her again. The feelings had crept up on her. They'd seen so much less of each other since the accident that her heart started to race as soon as she caught sight of Echo. She couldn't stop staring at her body, remembering every warm, responsive contour. It was as if they'd just met and she was still finding out who her lover was. Kyla couldn't decide how to deal with the feelings, so she was trying to ignore them.

"I'm serious," Echo said. "She told you herself there was nothing. She made it up. She admits that. I've never been unfaithful to you. Not once in eighteen years. I need to know you believe me. I need to know you feel you can trust me."

Kyla sat silently, gathering her thoughts before responding. "Echo, it's not just about Jenny. There are things you withheld from the investigation. There's your lack of interest in helping."

Echo shook her head. "But don't you see? Those are things you perceived. They're not real, baby. They're misconceptions based on the belief that you couldn't trust me because you thought I'd cheated on you. But I didn't. And you know that now."

"Okay, you have a point. But I can't just suddenly turn on the trust again. You'll have to be patient with me while I learn to take that for granted again."

"But I don't want you to have to *learn*. The other night, over dinner, you said you believed me when I made that promise."

"And I do," Kyla said. "But there's a feeling when you trust someone completely, and a wall in the way when you don't. I need you to understand that I can't just knock the wall down. It has to come down on its own."

"So I wait?"

"Well, I suppose we can move on as if the trust is there and I do my best to get past this."

"That's all I can ask for." Echo leaned down and brushed her lips across Kyla's. "Well, all I'll ask for right now."

Kyla sat quietly, listening to Echo's footsteps going downstairs. She closed her eyes and breathed a sigh of relief. That had gone better than she'd expected. She'd been dreading the inevitable conversation since the night before. The knot in her stomach hadn't completely unraveled, however. She still had to tell Echo about the strange man and her feeling that he might have been somehow connected to her shooting. She got the feeling Detective Magnell didn't buy it, and she felt Silverton was patronizing her. She couldn't guess what Echo's reaction would be, but either way, she had to tell her. Echo was Colton's mom, too.

Kyla threw on a pair of sweats and noisily clomped downstairs to get the next discussion over with.

"I didn't expect you down so soon." Echo turned away from the stove. "I was just getting breakfast started."

"Well, there's something else we need to discuss and I'd just as soon talk about it now."

"Can I talk and cook at the same time?"

"I'd rather you come sit at the table with me."

"Okay." Echo pulled out a chair. "What's going on?"

"I never told you why we came to the gym last night."

"No, you never did," Echo said gently. "I thought it was urgent."

"It was…is. I just wondered if I was overreacting." Kyla relayed the story to Echo, feeling the anger emanating from her as she told her of the apparent danger Colton was in.

"That's it?" Echo asked when Kyla told her the car drove off as the boys turned down Levi's street. "That's all the description Colton got of him?"

"I'm afraid so."

"And the scumbag seriously smiled before he drove off?"

"That's what Colton said."

Echo shook her head and stared out the window. Kyla watched her jaws clench and could sense every one of her muscles tensing and relaxing repeatedly. She could feel the anger and frustration effusing from every pore.

"You didn't tell me this last night, why?" Echo asked softly.

"I'm sorry, but once I saw…you and…her, I got angry and forgot why I was there in the first place. Then, when we got home, I started wondering if I was being melodramatic."

Echo nodded.

"There's something else I want to tell you."

Echo turned and focused on her. "There's more?"

"Well, it's a feeling I had. I really think he had something to do with the shooting. I don't think following Colton was random."

"What are you saying?"

"Just that. I have a feeling it's all connected."

Echo stood behind her and rubbed her shoulders. "How so? You weren't with Colton when it happened, were you?"

"No, I wasn't. So I didn't see the man. But I can feel it. I know it doesn't make any sense. But I feel it in my bones."

Echo sat back down and took Kyla's hands. "We've had a

lot going on lately, sweetheart. We've had our share of problems. And we've let the detectives handle the investigation. I think it's time that we put more of our own energy into figuring out what happened, okay?"

Kyla pulled her hands away. "You don't believe me either, do you?"

"It's not that I don't believe you. What I'm saying is that we need to explore this. We need to find out who the man is and what he had to do with the shooting. We'll renew our focus, babe, okay?"

Kyla nodded slowly. "Yes. I think it's time we took a more active role, too."

❖

Kyla watched the rain fall. She felt as dank and dismal as the February weather. Her whole world had fallen apart and she had no idea how to fix it. When the threat had only involved Echo and herself, it was hard enough. But now Colton seemed to be a target, she couldn't help but blame herself. On some levels she knew that wasn't logical, but she was also convinced that if she hadn't been shot, the man wouldn't be following Colton. Even if no one else believed her, she was certain in her gut. If only she could remember something about that horrible night, she might be able to prove that everything was connected. Then maybe this horrible mystery would be solved, her family would be safe, and life would be normal again.

"What are you doing?" Echo asked, joining her on the couch.

"Cursing the rain."

"Is that all you're cursing?"

"Not really. I'm cursing life in general right now."

"Are you trying to come up with any solutions? Or just basically cursing?"

"I'm having a pity party, Or rather, I suppose I have been having one. But Colton's in danger now, so I can't just sit here feeling sorry for myself."

Echo took Kyla's hands in her own and kissed them. "You're being way too hard on yourself."

"How do you figure?"

"Why do you say you've been having a pity party?"

"Because I've been sitting around feeling sorry for myself for not having all my memories, and whoever shot me has been running around scot-free. And now he's going after Colton."

"That hasn't been established yet," Echo said, adding when Kyla glared at her, "I'm just saying. Now, with no memory, how do you think you can help the investigation?"

"I should have tried harder to remember." Kyla pushed Echo away when she tried to offer comfort. "See? I let people do that. I let you coddle me, encouraging me to feel sorry for myself."

"There's a difference between offering comfort and coddling."

"The point is I could have done more and I haven't."

"No. The point is you went through a horrible ordeal, which resulted in you losing your memory. That's *not* your fault. And nothing could have changed that."

"Maybe you're right. *Maybe*. But what if I could have done more and by doing more, protected Colton? What if?"

"Again, we don't know that the man who followed Colton is the same person who shot you. But we *do* know that Colton is fine."

"How can you say that? Do you know how terrified he must have been?"

"True. But physically, he's fine. He's not shot. His car hasn't been totaled. He's not hurt. And that may just have been some freak who liked what he saw and took the opportunity to enjoy the view for as long as he could."

Kyla stared at Echo, wanting to believe her, feeling herself starting to believe. But still something held her back. "Surely there has to be something I can do to help the investigation. I don't understand why it's going so slowly. This is a small town. How many people own guns? Are they even interviewing anyone except you and me and our neighbors?"

"I know it's frustrating," Echo said. "But the cops are looking for this guy, and they'll find him. They usually do."

Kyla knew she was brooding and being unreasonable, but she hated feeling helpless, and every time she let Colton out of her sight, she felt sick with worry. "I don't want to take any chances."

"Relax," Echo said. "Colton will never be alone until they find the creep. You haven't done anything to endanger him. I'm off to work out now. Why don't you go take a nap?" She kissed Kyla and went downstairs.

Kyla sat fuming, still feeling like everyone was babying her and no one was taking her seriously.

❖

It was awkward and uncomfortable sitting in the master bedroom, but Kyla wanted to talk to Echo as soon as she got out of the shower. So she waited in the computer chair, trying to relax. Instead she looked longingly at the king-size bed she and Echo had shared and thought of the hours they'd spent making love there. Echo was such a skilled lover. She knew just where to touch, to kiss. And she was tenacious. She wouldn't rest until Kyla was completely satisfied.

Kyla squirmed in her chair, a different sort of discomfort taking over. She had been wanting to come back and sleep with Echo every night, but she had the plaster cast to contend with and she'd been uneasy about sending a signal. Returning to their bed would be an acknowledgment that all was well, and it wasn't as yet. She was so lost in thought that she hadn't noticed the shower was no longer running until Echo rounded the corner, towel-drying her hair.

"Sorry," she said, making no attempt to cover her nakedness.

"No, I'm sorry." Kyla was unsure where to look. "I should have let you know I was here."

"Why? It's your room, too."

Echo took a pair of boxers from her dresser. Kyla watched, mesmerized as first one long leg and then another slid into them, eventually covering the parts Kyla was craving.

"Well?" Echo prompted. "To what do I owe this unexpected pleasure?"

"Oh, right. I was hoping that we could go over that night again. Maybe see if I remember anything else?"

Echo slid an A-shirt over her head, hiding her small, firm breasts. "Wouldn't you know if you had more memories?"

"You'd think. But I've replayed the scenes so many times, I thought maybe if you could ask me questions, we could see what I come up with. Besides, you know the questions they asked me in the beginning, and to be honest, I don't really remember them. So maybe I do remember more than I did and I don't even know it. Was that in English?"

Echo laughed and sat on the bed. "Yes, actually, that was in perfect English. Where do you want to start?"

"I guess from the beginning."

"The beginning it shall be, then. Tell me what you remember about work."

"It was boring, as is usual for that time of year. It was Laura's birthday so we had cake at lunch. That's about it."

"You sure that's all you remember?"

Kyla flashed to the angry words she'd recalled in fragments. "There's something else, but I don't know what it means. I remember someone really pissed off asking, 'Did you really think you could get away with this?' But I don't know if I said that or if someone was saying it to me."

"See?" Echo encouraged her. "This is new."

"Not really. I just didn't mention it before."

"And you still don't have a context for those words?"

Kyla was silent for a moment before cautiously answering, "I think it was that Vasquez woman, wasn't it?"

"I can't answer that for you. Either you remember it or you don't. You can't just guess. That's not helping anyone."

"It was her. After you told me I'd fought with her, I racked my brain and I realized she called and sarcastically thanked me for costing her her job. I told her I didn't know what she was talking about. That's when she said that to me."

"She was still pretty caught up in that hurtful game then."

Kyla raised an eyebrow. "And you really believe she's not now?"

"I think the whole thing is over."

"I wish I shared your confidence." Kyla stretched out her leg and slid her finger under the edge of the plaster to scratch her irritated skin. "I've been wondering if she would have hurt me to get even for losing her job."

"Jenny Vasquez is a lot of things, none of which is stupid," Echo said dryly. "She cost herself that job and she knows it. Let's move on. Do you remember the drive home?"

Kyla shook her head. "You said we fought, but I don't remember that. I don't remember anything until I dropped Colton off."

Echo slid to the edge of the bed. "You remember dropping him off?"

"Of course."

"Do you remember picking him up to take him to lessons? Where was he?"

Kyla shook her head. "I don't remember."

"Think, baby. Think hard. You remember dropping him off, now backtrack. Where did you pick him up?"

"I really have no idea." Kyla looked longingly at the bed. Her body hurt and she wanted to lie down.

"That's okay. At least you remember dropping him off. That's a breakthrough. This is awesome."

"So my memory *is* coming back." Kyla stood and stretched. "Slowly but surely. If only it was less slowly and more surely."

Echo patted the bed. "You look tired. Come and lie down."

Kyla didn't feign reluctance. She let Echo help her up and collapsed gratefully into the pillows.

"Do you remember anything else about after you dropped him off?" Echo asked. "Anything at all?"

"I remember being on Bidwell Drive and crossing Oasis Avenue."

"Do you actually remember being on Monroe?"

"I do. Is that new?"

"It is. Now think, sweetheart. I hate to put pressure on you, but I really need you to think. How far along Monroe Drive do you remember being?"

Kyla shook her head, tears forming in her eyes. "I don't remember getting to Lone Pine."

"I don't think any of us expect that from you." Echo slid an arm around her shoulders and rocked her close. "Just picture yourself driving along."

Wiping away a tear, Kyla said, "I remember getting as far as Houston."

"That's not far from Lone Pine."

"But as soon as I crossed Houston something happened, Echo. I don't know what, but I don't remember anything after that."

"Kyla, baby, don't you see how incredible this is?"

"Well, I get that it's positive that I remember more now than I did before."

"It's way more than just positive. And to think that you have memories lurking just out of reach that could very well unlock this whole thing. Oh, sweetheart. I'm so happy for you. For us."

As in years past, Kyla allowed Echo's strength and confidence to wash over her. "It'll be so awesome to be able to remember everything."

She smiled into the blue eyes holding her own. Echo looked genuinely happy, far too happy for someone with something to hide. It came to Kyla in a flash of understanding that Echo also wanted to know who fired those shots. She wanted the case solved because she was blameless, and so far, Kyla had refused to believe that. Echo wanted to prove her and the detectives wrong. She was innocent. Only an innocent person would want Kyla to get her memory back.

"It's so good to see you smile again." Echo brushed Kyla's short hair off her forehead and quickly, lightly kissed her cheek.

Embarrassed by Echo's unfailing support and tenderness, Kyla tried to look away, but she couldn't make herself. She felt Echo's strong hands under her jaw and watched as her lips moved closer to her own, until she felt them kiss hers. She opened her mouth to welcome her partner's tongue. Lying on her back, feeling Echo's hands on her body, she allowed her mind to drift to happier times.

Echo raised herself on an elbow. "You're tired. Come to bed."

Shocked, Kyla realized she'd drifted into half-sleep while she was being kissed. Drowsily, she said, "Don't stop."

Echo laughed. "I'd rather you were awake when we make love. That's one memory I want you to have."

CHAPTER FIFTEEN

Echo was in a foul mood when she walked into the gym on Monday morning. She was frustrated on so many levels. She was still irritated at Jenny, not fully understanding what drove her to wreak the havoc on the life she'd had. She was frustrated over the investigation into Kyla's shooting. She was frustrated that Kyla was on the brink of trusting her again and accepting her as her partner, but was so worried for Colton's safety that her mind seemed to be elsewhere. And at the moment, Echo was sexually frustrated as well. Even in their darkest times, she and Kyla had made love at least three times a week. She wasn't used to going without. Add to that Kyla's sleepy teasing from the evening before, and Echo knew it was a day she should be left alone.

She was sitting at her desk, contemplating where to start when she heard footsteps in her doorway and her assistant knocked. "What's up, Meadow?"

"There was some weird guy here on Friday night."

Echo was fully focused. "A guy?"

"Yeah. I tried to get rid of him as fast as I could."

Echo waved her off. "Don't worry about that. Just tell me what happened."

"He came in right after you left. I'm telling you, he really creeped me out. He was asking a lot of questions about the gym and about you and Kyla. He knew about the shooting. He was asking how Kyla was doing, if she'd died. He even asked if she was a lesbian."

Echo tried to appear calm, even with her stomach cramped in fear. "What did this guy look like? Have you ever seen him before?"

Meadow shook her head. "Never, and I hope I never see him again. He kept looking around and asking if other women here were worried that they'd get shot, too."

"The guy seems to know a lot," Echo observed. "What did he look like?"

"Ugly. Dark hair, but he had a baseball hat on. And his eyes gave me the heebie-jeebies. They were, like, white."

"White?"

"Like really light, silvery green, almost white."

"Sounds handsome," Echo said with irony.

"Or not."

"I don't suppose you got a look at his car, did you, Meadow?"

"Sort of. It was hard because it was dark outside. All I could tell was it was a dark four-door."

"Any idea what kind of car it was?"

Meadow looked thoughtful. "You know, I didn't see any markings on it at all."

"Thanks for the info, Meadow. And thanks for getting the creep out of here."

"No problem. I just hope he doesn't come back."

As soon as she was alone, Echo called the police station and asked for Detective Silverton. They exchanged brief, polite greetings, then she asked, "Hey, you know that car that followed Colton home Friday? I think the guy was at the gym on Friday night."

"Did you see him?"

"I didn't, but Meadow gave me a description."

"I'll be there shortly."

Five minutes later, Silverton arrived at the gym and was interviewing Meadow.

Meadow relayed her story yet again while the detective scribbled notes. When she was through, Silverton told them she was going to release a description of the car to the media and ask everyone to be on the lookout for it. She handed each of them a business card. "If either of you see the car, please give me a call immediately."

Echo watched her drive off. Not having any idea where to start to find the dark car was just one more frustration to add to her growing list.

❖

Jenny Vasquez pushed her cart toward her car in the parking lot of Ferrini's, the lone grocery store in Bidwell. She jumped as a car sped by, shooting a spray of water in her direction. She raised her hand and flipped the careless driver off, and then was repaid when he stuck his hand out of his window, his own middle finger extended in a mutual salute. As she stared after him, she felt like she'd seen the car before but couldn't remember where. It wasn't until she was home with the evening news on that she knew why the vehicle seemed familiar. It was right there on the screen, its driver listed as a person of interest in an ongoing investigation.

While normally Jenny would have waited for Pat to call her after their shared dinner, this gave her the perfect excuse to make the first post-date move. She picked up the phone.

"I saw the car, Pat," she said as soon as Pat picked up. "The one on TV."

"You did? Where? Is it near you?"

"No. I saw it at the store."

"I'm on my way to get your statement."

"I'll be waiting."

Jenny took advantage of the fifteen minutes to touch up her makeup and brush out her silky brown hair. She stood in front of the mirror and admired her reflection. She still felt overdressed, and her clothes were damp from the car's splash. Quickly, she stepped out of the skirt and sweater she'd been wearing and slid into some black satin pajamas, strategically leaving the top button undone. She was finally satisfied with how she looked when she heard Pat's knock on the door. She stepped back to allow her guest in and watched as she took in her surroundings.

"Are you safe?" Pat asked.

"What if I say I'm not?" Jenny joked.

"This is serious, Jen," Pat answered as she checked the bedroom for any intruders.

"Jen? That's the first time you've called me that."

"Is that okay?" Pat called.

"It's great. I like it." She smiled for a moment. "So what's this ongoing investigation the car's involved in? I didn't know Bidwell had any of those."

Pat walked back out to the front room and stared at Jenny. "Nice outfit." She smiled.

"I thought you'd like it." Jenny moved closer, running her hands over Pat's chest. She searched Pat's face. Seeing the desire burning there, she brushed her lips across Pat's.

"What do you think you're doing?" Pat took a step back.

"I'm happy to see you," Jenny protested. "Just wanted to show you how much."

"I've got to stay focused," Pat said. "I need to get your

statement. This is part of a police investigation. So you have to be sharp, too. You can't forget any detail."

"And you think a couple of kisses are going to make me forget some greaseball flipping me off?"

"Okay, let's sit down and go over what happened."

As soon as they were on the couch, Jenny kissed Pat again, this time pressing her back hard against the couch. Pat pushed them both upright. "I mean it."

"Fine." Jenny stuck out her lower lip. "What do you need to know?"

"Everything," Pat said.

Jenny recounted the incident in the parking lot, ending with the man giving her the bird. "He was a real piece of work. And when he flipped me off, I could see some bright orange and red tattoo sticking out of his jacket."

"A tattoo?" Pat was excited. No one else had reported seeing that yet. "What did it look like?"

"I don't know. He was too far away by then. It looked like flames or something, but like I said, I didn't get a good look. And I'm sure I only saw part of it."

Pat stood up. "This is excellent information. Thank you so much."

"My pleasure." Jenny slid her arms around Pat's neck.

"What's going on?"

"You haven't even called me since dinner. You seemed to be enjoying yourself that night, and then I hear nothing."

"I *was* enjoying myself. You know that. But I also told you I need to solve this case. I need to show the world that you're above suspicion. And I still promise to do that. So I'm going to go back to the station with this new information and work my ass off so I can keep that promise, okay?"

She pulled Jenny close and kissed her, nibbling her lips.

Jenny held her tight and returned the kiss, sliding her tongue along Pat's lips. Pat opened her mouth to welcome her and held the back of Jenny's head while she roamed the moist warmth of her mouth.

When she broke the kiss, both women were breathless.

"You trust me now?" Pat breathed.

Jenny could only nod.

"Good. Then I'm going back to work." She kissed Jenny again, this time tenderly. "But I'll be back when we can finally take this where we want to go."

Jenny returned to the couch after she let Pat out and thought about their budding relationship. She absently unbuttoned her shirt and ran her hands along her full breasts. Her nipples were rock hard and felt wonderful as she ran her palms over them. She slowly teased them before cupping and kneading her breasts. She bit her lip and let out a slight moan. She needed Pat. It had been too long since she'd enjoyed a woman's company.

Sliding her hands down, she pushed her pajama bottoms off, then flopped a leg along the back of the couch. She pressed her fingertips into her clit, then spread her lips before plunging inside herself. With her free hand, she cupped her breast again and pinched her nipple while her fingers rapidly moved in and out of her pussy and her palm pressed into her clit. It wasn't long until she took herself to a powerful orgasm that lasted for several minutes. She lay there catching her breath, temporarily sated, but craving Pat Silverton more than ever.

CHAPTER SIXTEEN

That motherfucker!" Echo yelled, running down the stairs, past Kyla and throwing open the front door. Kyla heard the screeching of tires and the roar of an engine. She limped to the door in time to see taillights fading in the distance.

"That was him, wasn't it?"

"Yes. And he got away." Echo slammed the front door and flipped open her cell phone.

"Was he with him?" Kyla asked.

Echo paused, then closed her phone and slid it back in her pocket. "What did you just say?" She stared at Kyla who had a vacant look on her face.

"Was the little boy with him?"

"What boy, Kyla? What are you talking about?"

"The little boy from before," Kyla answered. "Was he with him?"

"You're not making any sense. Look, the scumbag was here. In our neighborhood. And I need to call the cops to report it." Echo grabbed Kyla's arms and shook her gently. "So explain what you're talking about, please. What little boy? Have you seen the car before? Why would a boy be with him?"

Kyla shook her head to clear it. "I just remembered something. I think it's important."

Echo ran her hands through her hair in frustration. "I've got to tell you, I have no idea what the fuck is going on. On second thought, wait."

She grabbed her phone again and called the police station. After receiving a promise from Detective Magnell that they were on their way, she turned her attention back to her partner, walking her back to the front room.

"Okay, tell me about the little boy."

Kyla hesitated only a moment. "I saw a man with a little boy that Friday night. They're connected. I'm sure of it."

"Like that feeling you had about the driver of the car?"

"And was I right. Otherwise why would he show up at the gym and our house?" Kyla was getting frustrated again.

"We have no proof. Kyla, think about it. Why on earth would a man with a kid shoot you?"

"I have no idea, but I hope we find out soon."

Their discussion was interrupted by a knock on the door.

Echo led the detectives to where Kyla was waiting in the front room.

"Hi, Ms. Edmonds," Detective Silverton said. "How are you feeling?"

"Much better, thanks."

"If it wasn't for her occasional irrational moments," Echo offered.

"Isn't that a drawback of living with a woman?" Magnell asked.

All three women looked at each other and rolled their eyes.

"Remember when the car followed Colton home?" Echo said. "She'd never seen the car. And yet she was convinced it was involved in her shooting or accident. And now, she *still* hasn't seen the car"—Echo shot a meaningful look Kyla's way—"but she's decided the man who drives it had a boy with him that night. Where the hell did *that* come from, I ask you."

"A little boy?" Silverton perked up and cast a glance at her partner, who looked like he was asleep with his eyes open. "What little boy, Ms. Edmonds?"

"Yes. There was a little boy with the man that night."

"Is there anything else you remember? Did the man shoot you? What was the boy doing?"

Kyla shook her head frantically. "I'm sorry. That's really all I can remember right now. It's so frustrating. I think it's worse to remember bits and pieces rather than not remember anything."

Pat decided to give her a break. She briefly knelt in front of her and patted her arm. "Don't beat yourself up. Every little bit of memory that comes back helps us, okay? We're trying to piece this puzzle together, and the more you can help, the better."

She stood and looked over at Magnell, who said, "A boy? That's all we got?"

Pat directed her attention to Flannery. "Why don't you take me through what you saw tonight?"

"I was upstairs in my room." She didn't appear to notice Pat's raised eyebrow. "I heard a car, looked out my window and saw it. I ran downstairs and opened the door just as he was completing his circle around the cul-de-sac."

"Did he see you?" Pat asked.

Echo nodded. "He pretty much came to a stop across the street and just stared at me."

"Did you see him?" Pat asked Kyla, who shook her head in response.

"I already told you that," Echo said.

"So you're still trying to speak for her," Magnell said.

"I'm not. I'm just saying she doesn't have to ask Kyla questions I've already answered."

"So you say."

"Can we please focus on what's important?" Echo glared at him.

"Did you see the car at all?" Pat continued with Kyla.

"I saw his taillights as he drove off. But I didn't see the car."

"Has anyone described this man to you? Do you have some idea what he looks like?"

"I heard Colton describe him to you."

"What about the boy? Do you remember what he looked like?"

"We're back to the boy?" Magnell lamented.

Pat ignored him. On a hunch, she took out a folded photocopy and spread out the Joey Andrews pic circulated in the last briefing. "Do you recognize this child?"

Kyla stared down at the image, then shook her head again. "I'm sorry. I don't know. He seems familiar."

"That's okay. You can keep the picture. Listen, we're going to find this guy. And then we'll find out what his interest is in your family. Try to enjoy the rest of your evening."

As they crossed the street to their car, Magnell asked, "Why the fuck are you encouraging that woman's delusions?"

"Who says they're delusions?"

"Really, are you serious? Some perv is driving around Bidwell. There is no, I repeat *no* reason to believe that perv is associated in any way to the shooting and accident, or to the Medford kidnapping. And now she's decided there was a boy who she doesn't remember with this man who she doesn't remember. Did it ever occur to you these could be byproducts of her pain meds? I'm telling you, this isn't a police investigation, it's a fucking witch hunt."

Pat sat down and strapped in and waited for her partner to do the same before speaking. "But what if? What if it *is* all connected? We owe it to her to look into it."

"It's a waste of the department's money."

"It's not. Policy is every lead gets followed until it's exhausted. That's what we'll do."

Pat didn't say out loud that the more places they looked, no matter how unlikely, the quicker this investigation would be complete. Once Jenny's name was cleared, she would be able to pursue the relationship she so desperately craved.

❖

Pictures were strewn across the desk in the old office. With the computer now set up in the master bedroom, this room was used more for storage than anything. And there were many photos stored in there that had yet to make it to albums.

Kyla knew she and Echo had been happy, really happy at some point. Her goal was to find pictures showing that. Granted, for the most part, Echo had been very supportive during her recovery. But it was the intermittent lack of assistance with the investigation that had made her question their relationship. She understood that better now, and she felt more certain than ever that Echo had simply been reacting to suspicion. Like any innocent person, she was angry to be treated like a suspect.

Kyla brought herself back to the issue at hand. She piled the shoeboxes on one end of the desk, reached in and grabbed a handful of photos, and spread them on the desk. There were only five shoeboxes, but that was enough to strengthen her resolve to get them all organized and in photo albums to go in the trunk in the master bedroom. As she'd expected, there were many photos of her and Echo together, and most just looked like typical couple photos. None looked particularly happy or unhappy, just like someone had said, "Say cheese." And they had complied. She picked up a particularly good snap of Echo. Who wouldn't want to go to bed with her? Obviously Jenny Vasquez had wanted to, even if nothing ever happened. Kyla shook her head, willing herself not to focus on that. Whenever she tried to figure out what the true story really was, she felt like a cat chasing her tail. Just when she thought she understood, she got confused once more.

Kyla started three piles: one where they looked incredibly happy, one where they looked somewhat happy, and one where they looked like they could barely hold their smiles long enough for the picture to be taken. The first pile was embarrassingly small. Yet Kyla still swore they had been very happy once upon a time.

The next handful she grabbed was of a party of some sort at a restaurant or bar with lots of smiling and happy people, but she didn't see Echo anywhere. She flipped to the next picture. Still no Echo. There was something familiar about the location, though. And she recognized a few faces. Some were former coworkers.

The next picture was of her, big smile, eyes half closed, leaning all over Brenda Dill, who hadn't worked at the firm in five years or more. Brenda was smiling as well and had her arm around Kyla. They almost looked like a couple. Kyla stared down at the image of Brenda, then dropped the photo like it was radioactive. Memories began to assault her.

She and Brenda were in the ladies' restroom that night and Brenda had told her she'd always been curious about what sex would be like with a woman. Kyla could tell she was drunk, and, tipsy herself, she'd told Brenda it was wonderful and slipped past her and out the door. The evening wore on with Brenda constantly smiling or winking at her. Eventually, with people getting up to dance or get drinks and others taking their places, Brenda ended up sitting next to Kyla, who was much more intoxicated by then.

"You're beautiful," Brenda whispered.

"You're drunk."

"I'd really like to suck a woman's nipple."

Kyla had felt a stirring between her legs. She'd been trying to ignore Brenda all night long, but the truth was she'd been very aware of where she was every moment since they'd met in the bathroom. "There are lots of women here. Maybe one of them will let you." She'd tried to sound nonchalant.

"But you have such nice tits," Brenda proclaimed, grabbing one of Kyla's, much to the enjoyment of the crowd.

Kyla felt her clit twitch and knew this woman was making her wet. She struggled for control. "Excuse me," she said, removing Brenda's hand and standing. She walked back to the restroom, hoping to clear her head.

When she heard the door close, she looked in the mirror and there was Brenda again, standing a few feet behind her. Brenda, with her short auburn hair framing her full, freckled face, was cute in an Irish maiden way. Her blue eyes twinkled in mischief, even while her body language gave away her fear and confusion. She closed the distance and wrapped her arms around Kyla's waist, holding her tight.

"Brenda, this isn't right." Kyla tried to fend her off.

"I've always had a crush on you."

"You're married."

"It doesn't count. You're a woman."

"So I don't count?" Kyla queried.

"That's not what I meant."

"But you're another woman. So it does count for me."

"You worry too much," Brenda argued before pulling Kyla's mouth down to hers.

Kyla tried to pull away, Brenda held tight. She gave up and allowed her a brief exploratory kiss before pulling back. "This isn't right. You can't do that."

She stormed out of the bathroom and felt completely discombobulated as she made her way back to the table. She was certain everyone knew what had happened, especially when Brenda slid into the booth next to her and tried for a close hug. At that point someone told a joke and Kyla laughed hard and leaned back into Brenda. She decided Brenda's full, soft figure was very comfortable, so there she stayed. Eventually they were rubbing each other's legs and holding hands and really enjoying their time together.

The party slowly wound down and Brenda and Kyla were among the last people there.

"I don't want to say good night," Brenda said.

"Neither do I."

"My Suburban is out there. Want to go talk for a while?"

"Okay," Kyla agreed, very drunk by then.

They stumbled to the car, in the back area of the parking lot, and climbed into the front seats, but didn't stay there for long. Brenda immediately kissed Kyla and soon her hands were roaming and the confines of the front area were too frustrating.

"Come on. Lie back here with me." Brenda led the way to the far back, where she lay down and unbuttoned her blouse.

When Kyla saw what she was doing, she was foggily aware that they'd crossed a line and she should leave. She reached for the door handle, but Brenda said, "It's okay. The windows are tinted, no one can see us. Now, come here."

She pulled Kyla on top of her and groaned as Kyla's hand found a bare breast. She then got Kyla's shirt open and sucked hard on her erect nipple. Soon, skirts were hiked up, panties were pushed down, and fingers were in and on each other until they were both exhausted from pleasure. As they lay there catching their breath, sanity seemed to dawn on Brenda.

"Oh, my God," she said as she put her clothes back on. "My husband better never find out about this. He'll kill us both."

"What? He's the really jealous type?"

"Yeah. Get dressed. You need to get out of here. I need to call him for a ride and you can't be here."

Kyla, while still very inebriated, was beginning to feel cheap and used. "Hey Brenda, I thought we could agree not to—"

"It doesn't matter. Let's act like it never happened." Brenda threw Kyla's panties at her, urging, "Go, just go."

"Fine, but remember *you're* the one who was begging for it all night."

"Whatever. You just remember he won't care about that. He'll kill us both. I swear to God, he'll kill us both."

"Okay, I'm out of here. I'll go over there and call Echo."

Brenda grabbed her arm. "Are you going to tell her?"

"Good God, no. Why would I?" Kyla was still a little drunk, but she wasn't completely stupid. She climbed out of the car as best she could and immediately called Echo, who said she'd be there in about twenty minutes. Brenda eventually figured her way out of the car, and even at a two- or three-car distance, Kyla could tell she'd been crying.

"Did you get hold of Rick?" she called.

"He's on his way."

"Good." Kyla felt it best they maintained their distance, just in case.

Eventually Echo pulled into the parking lot and halted next to her.

"Why are you parking? Let's go," Kyla said.

"Who's that?" Echo glanced at Brenda.

"A coworker."

"Is someone coming to get her?"

"Yeah, she's called her husband."

"Well, let's just wait till he gets here. You know, keep an eye on her."

"I'm sure she'll be fine." Kyla faced away from Brenda.

"It's almost two in the morning." Echo looked around. "Speaking of which, there really isn't anyone else around. Did you two close down the place?"

"What's that supposed to mean? We were talking and must have lost track of time, if you must know." Kyla noticed the questioning look Echo gave her but couldn't seem to shut herself up. On a defensive, whiny note, she said, "Okay, so I've had too much to drink. It's not a crime to go out by myself once in a while."

After another long look at her, Echo suggested, "Well, if you two are friends, why don't we go stand with her?"

"No!" Kyla spun around, panicked.

"Fine." Echo folded her arms and leaned against the car as well. "We'll wait here."

"I hope my husband never finds out," Brenda kept saying.

"What does she hope he never finds out?" Echo finally asked.

"I don't know. She's butt drunk. I'm sure her husband will be here any second. Can we go now?"

"Whatever *it* is," Echo continued, "Do you hope *I* never find out?"

Kyla laughed nervously and pretended not to hear her. Just then Brenda's husband pulled up and she gave him a big hug. He looked over at Echo and Kyla and thanked them for staying with her until he got there. Both couples pulled out of the parking lot, only one realizing something critical had happened that night.

The next morning Echo was waiting when Kyla made her way down the stairs, which she navigated gingerly, her head pounding. She sat at the kitchen table and gratefully accepted a cup of coffee. The first sip turned her stomach. The look on Echo's face turned it again. She searched her memory banks for what might have caused the look, but the search came up empty.

"How you feeling this morning?" Echo asked.

"Not good."

"No. I wouldn't imagine. You got pretty lit last night."

"I was. That's so unlike me."

Echo nodded. "Speaking of being unlike you, do you want to tell me what it is you hope I never find out?"

Kyla looked perplexed. "I can't imagine. Why?"

"Allow me to nudge your memory. I do believe it had something to do with a coworker who drives a Suburban?"

Kyla's stomach turned again. The idea of a Suburban made her start to shake. How much did Echo know? Kyla could barely piece together the events of the evening herself.

"Does it help if I tell you she doesn't want her husband to find out either?" Echo said.

Memories of the night came back, one unappetizing moment after the next: Brenda saying she was curious; Brenda kissing her; the two of them staggering out to the Suburban. The rest of the night was suddenly a complete and embarrassing memory.

"How did you know?" she asked quietly

"You were both a little too drunk to be sly about it."

"I am so sorry, Echo."

"I'm sure you are." They sat in strained silence. "Why,

Kyla? Why would you do that? And don't say because you were drunk."

Kyla thought she might be sick. Her head throbbed and the alcohol from the previous night combined with the morning's coffee and accusation to make her incredibly nauseous. She had no excuse for her behavior, but she knew Echo was waiting for an answer.

Echo offered, "She's a coworker, right? Is she someone you flirt with a lot at the office?"

"Brenda? Oh, God no." Kyla couldn't even imagine. "It was meaningless."

"Oh, I see. So she's not good enough for flirtation, but she was just fine to fuck last night?"

"It's not like that," Kyla said.

"Well, then how is it exactly?"

Kyla didn't know how else to put it. "She was hitting on me all night and I kept telling her no, but I suppose the drunker I got, the weaker my resolve got."

Echo's disappointment was palpable. "We're in a committed relationship. That means I make love only with you and you make love only with me. We made this commitment because we love each other. Our love should be strong enough to get us through anything. Our resolve should never weaken to the point that we forsake our love and allow another woman to touch us intimately."

"It wasn't like that." Kyla's voice cracked as tears formed.

"Either you had sex with her or you didn't. So yes or no, Kyla. Did you have sex with her?"

Kyla covered her face with her hands and, sobbing, simply nodded.

Echo sat quietly for the minutes it took Kyla to calm down. Then she sighed heavily. "I know you love me. I truly don't doubt that for a moment. And I want to trust you. But that's going to take some time."

"I understand."

"I hope you do." Echo stood and went into the kitchen. "The thing is, I *never* saw this coming from you. It never crossed my mind that you would cheat on me."

"I didn't mean to." As soon as she said it, Kyla realized how pathetic it sounded.

"The sad thing, I know what you mean," Echo said. "It wouldn't have happened if you hadn't gotten drunk. Do I need to worry every time you go out from now on?"

"I won't go out without you," Kyla said, full of contrition.

"That's not healthy."

"Well, I can promise you I'll never drink with coworkers again."

"That might be a good start. But somehow, you need to gain my trust back."

"What? Just tell me what I need to do and I will. Please. Tell me."

Echo shook her head. "Unfortunately, I don't know."

They sat at the table, Kyla focused on Echo and Echo focused on the floor. "I'm so sorry, Echo."

"I believe you," Echo said eventually, but her tone was injured and the hurt in her eyes was more than Kyla could bear. "You may even feel worse about this than I do. You have my love. You even have my forgiveness. But the trust will have to come with time."

Chapter Seventeen

Kyla came back to the present and sank into the overstuffed leather chair. It had been years since she'd thought of that horrid night. Jumbled thoughts tumbled through her head. How could Echo have forgiven her that easily? She must have known how out of character the fling was. And why couldn't Kyla forgive Echo the same way, even after Jenny admitted she'd made up the affair? Did she, on some level, feel it truly was in Echo's character to cheat? Did she think Echo had done this to get back at her? So many years later? But it turned out that Echo hadn't cheated.

Kyla thought of their conversation over dinner on Valentine's Day. She'd mentioned her feeling that Echo was keeping something from her. And Echo had said she didn't want to hurt her. Kyla had assumed Echo was referring to Jenny Vasquez, but she was no longer so certain. Had Echo chosen to say nothing about Brenda? Had she decided to spare Kyla's feelings and let her think she'd never strayed, that the betrayal in their relationship was entirely one-sided?

Another thought gnawed at the back of her brain. It was the way Brenda had kept insisting that if her husband found out, he'd kill them both. What were the chances he'd just found out? How violent was he really? Five years had passed and that encounter was ancient history. Was he the kind of male who would lose his mind regardless and envision a lesbian "predator" seducing his innocent little wife? Brenda had a child. By now he would be about six. Could that be the little boy she'd seen?

Stunned, Kyla considered the possibility that the shooting had nothing to do with Echo or Jenny, or anyone else except her. Perhaps she had brought this on herself. She grabbed her jacket and purse, and decided to go to Brenda and Rick's shop the next town over, where Rick engaged in his hobby of restoring old muscle cars. Kyla felt certain she'd find a dark four-door car when she got there.

She called Sierra to see if she could take her, and fifteen minutes later they pulled out of her side street and turned left on Monroe Drive. Kyla dug through her purse to be sure she had her cell phone, just in case. She rolled down the window to enjoy the warm late winter day. As they headed east, she saw a dark gray car heading west, coming right at them.

Each car slowed as they passed, and the driver of the gray car stared across, directly at her. He grinned an eerie grin and laughed a mirthless laugh. Gooseflesh erupted all over Kyla and she had no doubt she'd just seen the man who shot her.

"Do you know him?" Sierra asked. She stepped on the gas pedal as the other car flipped a U-turn and pulled in behind them.

"Drive," Kyla urged. "The police station. Get there as fast as you can."

They raced down the street, carefully watching the side streets for traffic while tracking the car in the rearview mirror. He kept pulling up and almost hitting them, but Sierra managed to speed up every time and stay out of his range. As they approached the intersection with Oasis, she pulled into the

Bidwell Police Department on the left and the man following them continued across the intersection.

Certain he wasn't coming back, Kyla got out of the car and balanced shakily on her crutches.

"Do you need me?" Sierra asked.

"No, I'll get myself home. Thanks." Kyla kissed her and hurried inside.

Detective Magnell came down the hall as soon as he was paged. "Are you okay, Ms. Edmonds? You look like you've seen a ghost." He took her by the elbow and led her back to his desk.

"I saw him," Kyla said.

Detective Silverton rose when they stepped into view. "Saw who?"

"I saw the car. And the man. He tried to hit me."

"When?"

"Just now. We were driving down Monroe."

"You're sure it was him?" Silverton asked.

"He looked just like they've all described him. Right to the baseball cap. And he laughed at me. Just before he turned around and followed me."

"So he knew it was you?" Magnell seemed genuinely surprised. He sat down.

Kyla nodded, then started to cry. "And now what? He knows my car. He can find me anytime."

"Detective Magnell will arrange for surveillance until we catch this guy," Silverton said. "Now, I have to ask. Did you recognize the man?"

"I told you. He looked just like everyone described him."

"What I meant was, have *you* ever seen him before?"

"No. This is the first time. But you could tell he knew who I was. And he seemed happy that I knew who he was, too."

Detective Silverton's phone rang and she listened briefly

before saying, "We'll be right there." To Kyla she said, "I'll drive you home while Detective Magnell follows us."

"I'm scared," Kyla said.

"You have reason to be," Silverton replied. "But think of it this way. You've flushed him out. We can catch him now."

Kyla shivered. "Please keep my son safe."

Magnell surprised her with the vehemence of his reply. "Don't you worry about that. Nothing's going to happen to your boy."

❖

The drive home went without incident, and once there, the detectives made a sweep of the house to be sure Kyla was safe. They asked that she call Echo and ask her to come home, then they waited until she arrived. Detective Magnell sat them down with polite ceremony. For once, he seemed to be paying close attention to them.

"Look, I understand we haven't always seen things eye to eye, but I really need you to listen to me," he said. "We've been busting our butts trying to find this guy you keep seeing and we keep striking out. We're going to demand extra manpower now, because not only is he just some creepy guy who shows up in odd places, he attempted to hurt Ms. Edmonds today by possibly rear-ending the car. That's attempted assault. I want you two to know that we are taking this very seriously. Do you understand?"

Detective Silverton added, "If either of you can think of anything, anything at all, that might be helpful, please call us anytime day or night."

Echo asked, "Is there anything we can do?"

"Yes," Silverton said. "Be careful. Keep a low profile.

Limit any time you spend out of the house. Take time off work if you can. Is Colton at home?"

"He's in his room," Echo said. "I picked him up on my way here."

"Doesn't this creep know where we live?" Kyla asked.

"We'll have a car cruising the neighborhood," Magnell said. "Unless you have any questions, we're going to take off."

As they let themselves out the door, Silverton added, "I want all doors and windows locked. This is no time to take chances. Be safe, and remember, we're just a phone call away."

❖

"Anything interesting on the news?" Kyla asked, sitting next to Echo.

It had been four days since the man had tried to hit Kyla and none of them had left the house. Colton spent most of his time playing video games, and Kyla and Echo alternated between watching television, reading, and trying to reconnect. If something didn't give soon, they were all likely to go crazy from cabin fever.

"I don't know. There's some big story breaking." Echo turned up the volume. "You know that boy from Medford who was kidnapped? I think they found his body."

"Oh, that's so sad. Why can't they ever find kidnap victims alive?"

"I don't think that's the way kidnappers work, babe."

"They take them from their parents, use them for their filthy needs, then throw them away like yesterday's trash. It's not right."

"No, it's not. Taking them in the first place isn't right," Echo pointed out.

"Where did they find his little body?"

"Hold on, babe. Here it comes."

They watched as the reporter, a blonde whose beauty couldn't be hidden by the hood of her raincoat, told the Portland metropolitan area that the little boy's body had been found in the small town of Bidwell. Echo and Kyla couldn't believe their eyes when the camera panned out and showed a grove of trees just down Monroe Drive, not far from where they lived. A group of coroner's employees were carrying a small body bag. The reporter went on about the body being found in the center of the grove, well off the street. She also said that the officials had yet to tell the media the cause of death.

A picture of the boy, a happy boy with a gap-toothed smile and messy brown hair, was suddenly on the screen, with the voice of the reporter running a constant narrative.

Echo felt Kyla tense next to her. "What is it, baby? What's wrong?"

"That's him."

"That's who?"

"That's the boy who was with that man."

Echo rubbed her temples, feeling a headache starting. "Kyla, really, it's beginning to feel like every time someone says something, it has to do with that night."

"Well, this time it does. That's the boy, and he died when he was shot in the stomach."

"What?" Echo turned to face her. "What are you saying? Do you remember this? Or are you speculating?"

Kyla glared at her before flipping open her cell phone and dialing Detective Silverton's number.

"Ms. Edmonds." There was panic in the detective's voice. "Is everything okay?"

"We're fine, Detective. Look, we were watching the news about that little boy they found up in the trees by Houston Street. I was wondering, can you tell me how he died?"

"I'm sorry, we're not allowed to disclose that information."

"Well, can you tell me this? Was he shot in the stomach?"

"Why would you ask that?"

"I remember, Detective," Kyla said. "I remember everything."

There was a short hush at the other end of the line and Kyla was sure she could hear Silverton letting out a long, slow breath. "Why don't you come down to the station, then, and tell us the whole story?" the detective requested.

Kyla stood up and reached for her crutches. "We're on our way."

❖

When Kyla and Echo were seated in the full, comfortable chairs at the detectives' desks, Detective Silverton faced Kyla. "You said you remember everything?"

"I'm sure I remember that whole night right up until I rolled the car and blacked out."

"That's great. Now, hold on a second. Echo, do you agree? Does she seem to have regained her memory rather than imagining things?"

"I don't know," Echo answered honestly. "I wasn't there that night, remember? I was working."

"I have no choice but to believe you, Ms. Edmonds. But

please bear in mind that we will have to verify everything you tell us."

"That's fine. I don't care. I just want to tell you what happened that night."

"Okay, then. Whenever you're ready.

"Well, the drive home from work was typical Friday traffic. I left early enough to miss most of it. I got to town and picked Colton up at his friend's. We drove the three or four blocks to his lessons. I dropped him off and ended up in the quagmire that is traffic in Bidwell. I remember thinking what a nice night it was and that had it been raining, the traffic would have been that much worse. Plus it was relatively warm for January. Not balmy, by any stretch, but warmer than the usual frigid temperatures.

"I crossed Oasis and drove on Monroe, heading to our house. As I approached Houston, I saw two figures crossing the street. It looked like a man and his son At first I thought it was cute how they were dressed the same, in dark jeans and sweatshirts with their hoods up. They were holding hands, although in retrospect, I suppose the man was dragging the boy."

"Just tell us what you saw," Magnell told her.

"When I was past them, I glanced in my rearview mirror and they didn't look familiar. That's odd for our neighborhood. We all know each other and our kids. But I'd never seen either of those two before, I was sure of it. By the time I arrived at Denton Drive, I'd convinced myself that something was amiss."

"What made you feel that way?" Silverton asked.

"I think I watch too many crime shows," Kyla confessed. "So I turned around and drove back down Monroe, thinking I was being foolish. I stopped directly across from them, rolled down my window, and asked if everything was okay. The little boy tried to pull away from the man and he screamed for help. He yelled, 'Stranger. He's not my daddy.'"

Kyla felt the blood draining from her face, leaving her lips numb. "I was frozen, shocked or something. I couldn't do anything but watch. The man had a gun. He shoved it in the boy's stomach and I heard these sickening pops. The little boy was on the ground. There was blood."

Echo knelt beside her, rubbing her back. "Baby, are you sure you're up to this? Do you need a break?"

"I'm fine," Kyla answered, but gratefully accepted a cup of water from Detective Magnell.

Echo backed away and let the detectives refresh Kyla with water and cookies. Never had she been so proud of her partner. She knew there was more to come in the recounting of events from that awful night, but already she was amazed at what she'd heard. Pride that Kyla had come through this ordeal warred with guilt that she'd had to do so alone. Echo hadn't been there to protect her. Even though she knew deep down that she wouldn't have been able to do anything, she still felt the overwhelming desire to have shared the terror and somehow to have spared her partner the worst of it.

While Echo had known on some level that whatever had happened that night had been unimaginably horrible, she had never imagined that the love of her life had witnessed the killing of a child. She wanted to hold Kyla, comfort her, take her home to keep her safe. She loved her so much. She only hoped that Kyla would now allow herself to be loved and that they would get back to being the strong couple they truly were.

She longed for a return to the days when she could wake up in the morning and reach out to her partner, drawing her close. She loved the feel of Kyla's body just before she fell back to sleep. Of course, it was even better just as they woke up, both excited to show the other how much she was loved.

Giving in to the urge, she walked over and kissed Kyla hard on the mouth, then knelt down beside her again to hear the rest of the story.

"What happened next, Ms. Edmonds?" Magnell asked, apparently unfazed by the same-sex kiss. "Were you still parked across the street?"

"I was. I still felt like something was holding me in place, like if I stared hard enough I'd find out it had been an illusion or something. But it wasn't." Kyla paused, seeing the imprint in her mind so starkly it was as if there was no wear to the memory. Nothing had been altered through frequent recollection. Everything was as crisply detailed as a movie.

"I felt like I was in a trance, like I should turn away, but couldn't. I finally snapped out of it when I realized he was pointing the gun at me. I floored my gas pedal, but the car didn't move as fast as I needed. I didn't hear the shot, but I felt the bullet hit me just above my left ear. I was determined to get to the police station, even though I was starting to get really tired. I told myself to keep driving, but about the time I got to the Lone Pine development, I lost the battle. I woke up with my car against the giant pine and no recollection of anything. You know the rest."

"Are you sure the man you saw following you is the same one you saw that night?"

"I am. And that little boy is the one they just found. I recognized him in the photo Detective Silverton gave me, but I couldn't place his face until now."

"Your eyewitness testimony is going to be critical, so you need to be sure," Silverton said.

"I've never been more sure."

"It was dark that night," Magnell challenged. "How can you be so positive?"

"There's a streetlight right there between Houston and Denton. They were both well lit and very visible."

"You said they had hoods on."

"The boy's fell off when he looked at me."

"I just need to be sure," Magnell said.

"I'm sure. You need to trust me." Kyla felt incredibly sad. She'd seen the child alive. If only she had been able to do something. "What's his name?"

"Joey Andrews," Magnell said gruffly.

Before he said anything else, Pat said, "Well, you two get home. Be careful getting there. Be vigilant. You haven't had any problems, right?"

"None," Echo answered.

"And your son is fine?"

"We don't let him leave the house."

"That's what we like to hear. Nothing personal, Echo, but I'd guess either Kyla or Colton would be his next target."

"Well, he can't have either one of them," Echo said. "And if he tries—"

"You'll call us." Silverton smiled. "We're going to find him. Don't take any chances in the meantime."

CHAPTER EIGHTEEN

"They were pretty adamant about him coming after us, weren't they?" Kyla asked.

"Well, think about it. If he hears that you've got your memory back, he's going to be gunning for you."

"But that wouldn't affect Colton."

"No. I think Colton's fairly safe, or I never would have left him alone this evening."

"But this creep likes boys?" Kyla couldn't hide her nervousness.

"Colton's a lot older than that boy you saw him with," Echo said.

"Yeah. I suppose you're right."

They walked up to the front door and Echo slid the key in. The handle turned too easily. They looked at each other in fear.

"Are you sure we locked it?" Kyla asked.

"Of course I'm sure. I wouldn't leave Colton home without the door locked."

Together, they yelled, "Colton?"

There was no answer. Kyla started for the stairs but Echo grabbed her. "Wait. Don't go up there without me. Wait here while I check downstairs."

Kyla followed her to the top of the stairs and continued to call for Colton.

"He's not there," Echo gasped out. "Now let's go upstairs."

They took the stairs two at a time and raced to Colton's room. Music was still coming from his earphones, which were lying on the floor. They had never known Colton to leave his equipment in disarray. He was meticulous about caring for his possessions.

The women looked at each other, reality sinking in.

"Oh, God, Echo. He has him, doesn't he? He's taken Colton."

"We don't know that for sure. Stay calm." Echo grabbed her cell phone and dialed Colton's number. They heard the ring tone in his room.

"Oh, my God. He's gone!" Kyla fell to the floor and hugged herself, sobbing loudly. "Echo. He took him. That scumbag took our baby. We have to get him back. What are we going to do?"

Echo sat next to her and pulled her into her arms. She held her close and tried to comfort her, all too aware that every second of comforting was time away from finding Colton. She tried not to let Kyla feel her fear. "We need to report this."

Kyla struggled to stand and was happy to have Echo there to lean on. As they walked past the master bedroom, they saw their mirror had the word CUNTS written across it. Kyla started crying harder, so Echo steered her downstairs and out to the car. As they walked, she was on the phone to the detectives.

"How can you be so calm?" Kyla asked once they were driving.

"Inside I'm churning. But in case he's watching, I don't want to give the son of a bitch the satisfaction of seeing me upset."

They parked in the front of the station and walked inside, going right past the sergeant on desk duty, ignoring his admonishments. They strode down the hall, Kyla's plaster thudding loudly. The detectives were studying a map on a far wall, their backs to Kyla and Echo. They walked up and tuned into the discussion.

Silverton pointed to the map. "He's right here."

Magnell sounded disgusted. "I can't believe that slimeball has been living at the old Fabian house since that night Edmonds was shot."

"The old Fabian house? Off Monroe?" Echo asked.

The detectives spun around. "What are you two doing here?" Magnell asked.

"I was just leaving," Echo said.

"Echo!" Kyla cried, certain of where her lover was headed. "Don't go. It's not safe. Stay here."

"No, you stay here and talk to the detectives."

"You need to stay, too. Please, Echo."

"I have places to go. I need you to trust me on this." She kissed Kyla good-bye, ignoring the protests of the detectives. They could hear her tires squeal as she pulled out of the parking lot.

"Let's get out of here," Silverton said, putting on her Kevlar vest. "Does Echo have a gun?"

"Not that I know of." Kyla cast a glance around the room. Everywhere she looked officers were breaking out weapons and donning bulletproof vests.

"I hope you're right." Magnell loaded cartridges into his belt. "If she decides to take matters into her own hands, it could be ugly."

"Please." Kyla felt helpless and frantic. "We have to get there before he hurts Colton."

The detectives exchanged uncomfortable looks. "You

should stay here," Silverton said gently. "You'll be safer, and he'll need you once we extract him."

"Absolutely not," Kyla said. "I'm going, too. My son might be there."

"It will likely be unsafe for a civilian," Magnell told her.

"Then you can leave me locked in the car until that creep is in handcuffs. My baby's there and my partner's there. I'll be damned if I'm going to stay here."

"We don't have time to argue. Come on," Silverton said.

❖

Echo hated to waste any precious time by stopping, but she knew she needed to pick up the gun she'd just purchased. Once that creep started showing up all over the place, she'd bought a sidearm, just to be safe. When she got to the house she raced upstairs, her heart pounding noisily. She grabbed the gun from beneath the mattress, loaded it and grabbed spare cartridges, then sped off to the old Fabian house.

The house was small, and Echo guessed it had a living room, a tiny kitchen, and two bedrooms. There was also a one-car garage. What she didn't know was where the man was or where he was keeping Colton—assuming they were even there.

She parked the car a couple of blocks away so she could hopefully walk down undetected. The gun fit well in her hand and she checked to make sure the safety was off. She crept down the embankment that surrounded the house and was soon at the back door. Part of her wanted to find Colton and get him out of there, and part of her wanted to just find the greaseball and take him out.

The neighborhood was eerily quiet, and she felt that the sound of every twig she snapped echoed throughout the area.

As stealthily as possible, she picked her way down the side of the house, carefully looking into the bedroom windows. She still saw no human, which brought her conflicting relief and frustration. Peeking through another filthy window, she could make out the empty kitchen and living room, but couldn't see any sign of movement.

She finally arrived at the front of the house. The front door was solid wood, offering no way to see in. The front window's curtain was closed, also, so she stood there, pondering her next move.

"You think you're so tough, sitting there like that?" Echo heard a man yell inside. "I'll show you tough."

Echo braced herself but still wasn't prepared for the horrendous crash that emanated from the living room. She lunged for the door but thought better of it. She rubbed her forehead with the back of her hand. Her son was in there. She needed to get in and save him. But rushing in blind could get them both killed. Echo was not used to feeling powerless and didn't plan to stay that way for long. She stalked back around to the kitchen window and surveyed the interior again. The man's red baseball cap stuck out, so she focused her attention on it until he was completely visible, along with the baseball bat he was holding. She strained her eyes and finally saw Colton backed into the far corner. She knew what she had to do.

Echo raced around to the front and checked the door. It was unlocked, so she threw it open and burst into the room, gun trained on the man in the hat, who immediately dropped his bat and pulled his gun. Echo cursed at her slowness for allowing that to happen. Now the two of them stood across the room, guns pointed at each other. Fortunately, Colton was off to the side. He had slid down and was cowering in his corner, fear for his mother evident on his face.

The man sneered, "Big bad dyke. What the fuck do you think you're doing here?"

"I'm going to take my son home, for starters," Echo snapped. "Then I'm going to make you pay for what you did to the woman of my dreams."

❖

"Can't you drive any faster?" Kyla complained from the backseat. She pointed and yelled, "That's my car. Right there. Echo's here."

Magnell pulled the car in just ahead of Echo's. He turned around and told Kyla, "You need to stay in the car. We'll go see what's happening and advise the backup vehicles. We'll get everybody out of there safely and then you can see them. Do you understand?"

"Of course," Kyla answered,

The detectives grabbed their guns and quickly approached the house. So intent were they on their destination that they didn't notice Kyla following them at a distance. When they reached the house, Magnell looked through the window on the kitchen door while Silverton circled to the kitchen window. She immediately saw the standoff in the living room.

Rushing to Magnell's side, she said, "They're in the front room. I didn't see Colton, but Flannery and the kidnapper have weapons drawn. The front door looks open." She pointed to the side with the bedrooms. "Let's take that approach. I'm pretty sure there are windows over there, so we can keep an eye on them as we circle."

"Who's facing where?" Magnell asked.

"Flannery is facing this way. The kidnapper is facing the door."

"Maybe we should enter from back here," he suggested.

"At least this way we'd have Flannery facing us instead of him."

"True. And we're going to surprise them both. I just wonder who's less likely to panic and shoot."

"I still think Flannery's our best shot."

"Best shot for what?" Kyla asked.

They both turned.

"What the fuck are you doing here?" Pat Silverton asked.

"I couldn't wait in the car."

"Well, we can't babysit a cripple. We've got jobs to do," Magnell said. "So stay as far away from the house as you can. I mean that." He turned to Silverton. "Are you ready?"

"I am. I say we both rush in and take out the scumbag."

"Agreed. On three, I'm going to open the door. One… two…three!" He threw the door open and they both burst in.

"Police!" Silverton called. "Drop your weapon."

The man swung around and pointed his gun, first at one, then the other.

"Drop the gun," Magnell boomed.

"I'll shoot you, you sick bastard," Echo threatened from behind the kidnapper.

He edged back, glancing at the door. She slowly made her way in front of it, blocking his escape route. She tightened her grip on the gun. She was getting nervous and her palms were sweating. She couldn't let this creep get away, but she also wouldn't let him near Colton. She would stand her ground, but she sure wished the cops would do something to get his gun away from him.

"Sir, you need to drop the gun," Silverton said calmly.

"Drop it!" Magnell yelled again, with even more menace. "We *will* shoot."

He had barely uttered the final warning when the man opened fire at him, and Magnell returned fire as he took cover behind a cabinet. Colton covered his head with his hands, while the kidnapper looked confused in the commotion. He had his back to Echo. Without pausing to consider the risks, she charged across the room and kicked the gun out of his hand.

He spun around and swung at her. She leaned back so he barely grazed her chin, then punched him in the gut. He went down hard, like the flabby coward he was. Magnell and Silverton ran over and pointed their guns in his face.

"You got him?" Magnell asked.

Silverton nodded and cuffed the kidnapper, placing him under arrest. As she read him his rights, Echo ran over and scooped Colton in her arms. "Are you okay, baby?" she asked him as Kyla stumbled through the doorway, heading straight for him.

Throwing her crutches aside, Kyla took him from Echo and held him close. Almost as tall as she was, he wrapped his arms around her and laid his head on her shoulder, burying his face in her neck. He cried then, jagged sobs that tore at Echo's heart.

Magnell patted the suspect down, looking for weapons or other sharp objects. He took his wallet from his pants and read, "Timothy Daniels, huh? What exactly are you up to this evening, Mr. Daniels?"

"This kid showed up here, lost."

"That is so not true. You came and got me," Colton said.

Magnell yanked Daniels to his feet.

"He didn't touch you, did he, Colton?" Echo asked.

He shook his head. "No, but you gotta see his garage."

The adults looked at each other. Echo knew her face mirrored the same horrified anticipation she saw in the others. She didn't want to let her thoughts invent nightmares that would haunt her whether she saw the garage or not, so she said, "Let's do this."

Colton led the way as Magnell shoved Daniels in a staggering gait. "There's only one lightbulb." Colton flipped the switch, and a single bare bulb that dangled from the ceiling flickered to life.

Echo took in the musty space. Already the evening chill was creeping into the room. A row of card tables was set up in front of a large television. Each table had a console on it: PlayStation, Xbox, Nintendo. One had a laptop on it.

Silverton turned her flashlight on and shined it around the rest of the garage as they explored. There were three old army cots with very thin mattresses and no blankets. Closer inspection showed belts and wrist cuffs. Along one wall was a shelf that had paddles and lubes on it. The garage was clearly a place to lure teenage boys. They could play top-of-the-line games before Daniels had his way with them.

Pat used her phone to call for more officers to come down, take pictures, and collect more evidence. When she hung up, she asked Colton, "Did you go into any other rooms?"

"Just the front room. Where I was when you guys got here."

"Okay, well, I'd appreciate it if you and your moms would go wait in the vehicles. This is a crime scene and we need to secure it, so the less people wandering around, the better."

She and Magnell entered the house from the garage and walked down the hall toward the bedrooms. The first appeared empty except for another army cot. The master bedroom at the end of the hall had a bunk bed, two beanbag chairs, a television, and a dresser. A Polaroid camera sat on the dresser, as well as several digital cameras.

An inspection of the drawers turned up mostly men's

clothes with some young boys' clothing mixed in. These were mostly underwear and superhero pajamas.

"You are one sick bastard," Magnell said, jerking Daniels back to the other bed room.

Silverton opened the closet door. "Kids' toys," she noted. "Pirate ships, stuffed animals. Possibly a castle."

"Your victims like these toys, Daniels?"

"I didn't have any *victims*."

"No? What'd you call them, then? Little buddies? What?"

"I don't appreciate your tone," the man answered in a nasally voice.

"This is gross." Silverton inspected the cot. A urine-soaked mattress with a belt and cuffs on it would be a DNA fest.

"This where you buddies slept?" Magnell started on Daniels again. "They weren't victims, huh?" He held up a belt. "Is that why you have to force them to stay? Force little kids? Does that make you feel like a man?"

"I had the perfect one. He was perfect. But *she* fucked it all up. She couldn't just mind her own fucking business. She had to meddle. Stupid bitch."

"What are you complaining about?" Silverton shrugged, hoping to provoke a confession. She made sure the recording device in her pocket was on. "The *perfect one*? What a joke. As if you'd be able to attract that kind of kid."

"You don't know what you're talking about," Daniels threw at her. "I had my pick. Dozens."

"What was so special about Joey?" Magnell casually picked up on his cue. "Aren't all six-year-olds the same?"

"Not Joey." Daniels actually started blubbering. "He was completely unspoiled. Not one of those brats that wants everything when they give back nothing."

Pat decided the rest of the interview could take place at the station. Daniels had just admitted to knowing the child he'd murdered. He was going away for life. The rest was paperwork.

"Why here?" Magnell asked. "Why this house?"

"It was my mother's." Daniels sneered. "I'm surprised you were smart enough to find me."

Magnell shook him by the handcuffs, "You think you're so smart, dirtbag? You need to hurt little boys to make you feel big, and you think you're smarter than us?"

"Let's get him out of here," Silverton said. "Put him in a squad car with a cage." She took a final look around the room and stepped out into the fresh evening air with a heavy heart.

Echo, Kyla, and Colton were leaning against the car as though they, too, needed the cleansing chill of the outdoors. "We can feel safe for the first time in weeks," Kyla said as Pat reached them. "Thank you so much. For believing me. For never giving up."

"For everything," Echo said, holding her family to her.

Chapter Nineteen

Pat Silverton stood under the hot water trying to scrub the disgust of the house and garage off her. She might not have seen many child molestation cases, but she knew enough to know that Daniels was a repeat offender, and if he'd bragged about "dozens" there could be hundreds. She couldn't stop wondering about that, wondering where else he'd taken little boys and how many of them had escaped with their lives. Why had he chosen Joey?

Something about the case intrigued her more than most. She really wanted to understand how Timothy Daniels's mind worked. The more she thought about it, the filthier she felt and the harder she scrubbed. Thirty minutes later, skin raw, she finally stepped out of the shower and grabbed a black towel. One of the few luxuries she afforded herself were her extra-fluffy, oversized bath sheets. She dried herself off and then threw the damp towel over the shower rod. Her apartment was secluded, so she didn't bother with clothes. She helped herself to a beer from the fridge before playing one of her favorite Bonnie Raitt CDs. She sat on her beat-up couch, put her feet on her scratched green coffee table, and took a long pull on her beer. Head back, eyes closed, she waited for the usual calm to settle in. But it eluded her.

Restless, she stared at her weight set, but a workout didn't interest her. She checked her clock. It was nine thirty. She knew what she had to do to take the edge off. Filled with a different sort of anxiety, she put on her most faded jeans and an Oregon Ducks sweatshirt. Her favorite hiking boots and leather jacket completed the ensemble.

Her truck was parked in front of her apartment and she quickly climbed in and drove the now-familiar route to Jenny Vasquez's apartment. She parked in the lot and wondered briefly if she should have called first. Telling herself that one moment was as good as another if she was dropping by without warning, she took a deep breath and got out of her truck.

Jenny already had the door open when she got there and stood with a small smile on her face, staring at her.

"Won't you come in?" she asked and stood back.

Pat slid her hands in her pockets. "You look very nice tonight." She smiled broadly. Jenny was dressed in red satin pajamas. She looked edible.

"Why, thank you," she replied. "I wasn't expecting company."

"I'm sorry." Pat was suddenly serious. "Is this a bad time?"

"Don't be silly. I'm very happy you're here." She gestured toward the couch. "Have a seat. Can I get you a beer?"

"A beer would be great. Thanks." Pat folded her jacket over the arm of the couch and sat in the middle. "Do you always wear satin pajamas?" she called.

Jenny padded out carrying the beer and a glass of wine for herself. She snuggled next to Pat, handing her the bottle. "Always."

"Nice sweatshirt," she said, tracing the word *Duck* on Pat's breast.

Pat held her breath. The feel of her touch was just the kind of contact she was craving. Human contact. Normal, healthy human contact. Only she truly craved so much more from this woman. "I'm glad you like it."

"What would you do if I was a Beaver fan?" Jenny asked, referring to the rivalry between the two biggest universities in Oregon.

"I like beavers, too," Pat grinned, "but when it comes to sports, I'm all about my Ducks."

Jenny's eyebrows lifted. "So that's how it's going to be, huh?"

"What do you mean?"

Jenny smiled a tempting smile. "If you're going to play innocent, then so will I."

Pat situated her arm on the back of the couch and absently played with Jenny's hair. She knew where she wanted to end up and was pretty confident about how to get there. However, how to start the journey seemed like the greatest mystery of all time. She forced herself to say something.

"How have you been, Jenny?"

"I'm doing okay. How about you?"

"Life's looking up for me."

Jenny turned to face her. "Really, why's that?"

"Well…" Pat traced Jenny's jawline with her fingertips before pulling her close and tasting her lips. "We solved that case tonight."

After setting down her glass, Jenny threw her arms around Pat and held her tight. "That is such good news."

"Tell me about it. I was beginning to wonder if that would ever happen." She lay back on the couch and pulled Jenny on top of her. "So, we now know who it was and it wasn't you."

She kissed Jenny's neck, first tenderly, then in playful nips.

Jenny framed Pat's face and kissed her hard on the mouth. Pat's whole body was on fire when she felt Jenny's tongue slip into her mouth. She let her hands roam the satin that covered Jenny's back before sliding to the front and rapidly unbuttoning the shirt so she could cup her full breasts.

"Oh, God yes," Jenny moaned, struggling out of the shirt. She moved forward on Pat and dangled her breasts over her mouth. Pat licked first one, then the other before pressing them together and alternately sucking her hardened nipples.

She pushed Jenny back until she could lie on top of her. Pat quickly peeled the pajama pants off and kissed down Jenny's stomach to where her legs met. She gazed longingly at the wet, swollen area before dipping to taste it. She sucked on Jenny's coated lips, then allowed her tongue to dance inside. Jenny's clit was so swollen that Pat had to lick its length over and over before taking the head in her mouth and sucking hard while her tongue continued to stroke.

As Jenny frantically moved against her, she slid her fingers inside and pumped hard and fast, in time with her tongue. Jenny reached down and grabbed her free hand, creating just one more connection. She held tight as she bucked and the sensations came together, sending her barreling over the edge into orgasm after orgasm. When she could breathe again, she asked, "So we get to do this as much as we want now, right?"

Pat laughed. "As much as we like."

As she rested her head on Jenny's thigh, she realized that this was exactly what she needed to get her mind off the day. At least until tomorrow.

❖

Tom Magnell fought the bile in his throat as he pulled into a curved gravel driveway and let the car idle. He and his wife had called the restored farmhouse in west Bidwell home since they'd moved to town. He still felt sick from the sight and stench of the old Fabian house, and the feeling wasn't likely to go away soon. The end of that case had taken an unpleasant and unexpected turn. The surprise of what had really happened to the Edmonds woman that night in January had caught Tom off guard and opened some wounds he preferred to conceal.

"Shit," he muttered to himself when he reached the end of the driveway and saw three other cars there. All he wanted was a little peace and fucking quiet, and the whole family was here.

He sat in the car for a moment, bracing himself for the chaos that certainly reigned supreme in the house, with the three kids and their spouses and children. It wasn't that he didn't love them. He did. It was just that he wasn't up for interacting with them after the day he'd had. And he was definitely not in the mood for the memories.

But Tom couldn't spend the rest of the night in his car, so he made himself enter the house with his usual saunter, greeting those in his path with kisses to the cheek and pats on the head.

His twenty-nine-year-old daughter was in the kitchen with his wife. After he'd hugged her, he said, "I'm going to my office."

"But, Tom," his wife protested, "all the kids are here."

"I'm aware. For now, I'm going to my office."

He escaped through the house, careful to avoid the rest of his family. His office, his sanctuary, wasn't decorated as heavily as it had been when they still lived in Seattle, but the farmhouse was more open and airy, so he had furnished accordingly. The credenza and desk were both ash, and his desk chair was brown leather. He closed the door behind him and grabbed a decanter of bourbon as he crossed to his chair.

He poured himself two fingers and downed it. He sat in his chair and did it again. He hated cases like the one they'd solved that evening. No kid should ever endure what those kids did. And with him it was personal. He poured another drink.

A small boy ran into his office. "Hi, Grandpa."

"Out of my office," he said gruffly, more gruffly than he intended.

The youngster looked like he might cry as he turned and ran out, leaving the door creaking behind him.

"Shit." Magnell poured another drink and got comfortable in his chair.

His door opened again and he scowled to see his wife standing there. Still an attractive woman, she had aged gracefully. Her hair was gray, but she kept it short. Her hazel eyes still sparkled, whether in fun or when reprimanding him. They'd been married for thirty years; he couldn't imagine having spent those years without her.

"What?" he barked.

Ellen wiped her hands on her apron and crossed to stand in front of his desk. "What was that all about? You've got poor Jimmy in tears. He's only four, Tom."

He leaned his head back, closed his eyes, and whispered, "Holy Christ."

"What?"

"All I wanted was some time alone."

"Thomas, I don't buy that. I mean, I'm sure you did, but why yell at one of the babies?"

"I've had a rough day."

"I'm listening."

"You know that shooting case we've been working? It all broke open this evening."

"Did you get the guy?"

Tom nodded.

"Well then, shouldn't you be happy?" She sat in the chair across from him.

He poured himself another shot.

"How many have you had?"

"Enough." He strolled to the window and looked out at the trees. "The case ended at some piece-of-shit child molester's house."

"Tom, you're not supposed to be on those cases."

"It all happened at once. We had the lead on the shooting and one of the women was taking matters into her own hands. Their son was in the house and we had to go deal with the situation." He emptied his glass.

"So you didn't know?"

"Of course I didn't know. I mean, I knew the creep that lived there was a little weird, but I didn't know. Christ, Ellen, if you could have seen the place—" He turned quickly and looked at her. "Actually, God forbid you ever see anyplace like that."

She nodded. "I understand."

"It was horrible. Awful. Filthy. Disgusting. And all I could think was that Tommy was in a place like that. And we don't know if it was for a day, a year, or a decade."

"Tom, don't do this."

"We never found him. What the hell kind of dad am I that I let my little boy end up in a disgusting hellhole like the one I was in today? I was a detective in the Seattle PD, for Christ's sake."

"You couldn't have done any more than you did. He was grabbed from kindergarten."

"I know that, in theory. And I'm not supposed to get assigned to crimes against children cases, but what if I stumble across another situation like tonight? I don't know if I can handle it, Ellen."

"Hopefully that's not something you'll have to worry about."

"'Hopefully' isn't enough anymore. I think it might be time to retire."

"You know I'll support you in whatever you decide," Ellen said. "For now I'll leave you to your thoughts. And I'll try to keep the kids out of here."

"Thanks." He poured himself another drink and sat down, so lost in his tangled thoughts he didn't hear her leave the room.

CHAPTER TWENTY

S aturday morning, Kyla stretched languidly in bed, aroused slightly by the feel of the satin sheets on her bare skin. She rolled over, smiling as she thought of the previous night's lovemaking.

She felt Echo's arm wrap around her, sliding under her breasts. She nibbled Kyla's shoulders. "Do you know how much I love you?"

Kyla rolled back and slid her arms around Echo's neck. "I have some idea, but maybe you could show me."

"Show you?" Echo sucked her neck from one ear to the other.

"I'm getting the idea," Kyla whispered.

Echo kissed down her chest and licked her from nipple to nipple before taking one in her mouth and sucking it hard while her hand moved lower, slipping between her legs.

Kyla spread her thighs wider as Echo's fingers slid inside. "Oh yes," she moaned. "That's it."

Echo kissed back to the other breast and licked, long, lazy strokes while she moved faster inside her.

"Oh, my God, you make me feel so good." Kyla dug her heels in and pushed upward to meet the irresistible pulse of pleasure fast overtaking her. "I've missed you so much."

"I always want to make you feel good." Echo slid her fingers out and stroked the length of Kyla's swollen clit. "Do I love you?" she asked, before sucking again.

"God, yes," Kyla answered.

"You sure?"

"Yes. Yes. Oh, God, Echo."

Licking Kyla's nipple while she stroked her, Echo asked again, "Do you know how much I love you, Kyla?"

"Yes!" Kyla screamed. "Yes! Yes! Yes!"

Echo rubbed her just how she liked it and was rewarded with a deafening scream as Kyla grabbed her hand and held it to her. When Kyla's body relaxed and her breathing slowed, Echo pulled her close again. "Are you okay?"

"I'm fantastic." Kyla laughed. "Spoiled. Sated. Sweaty. What more could a woman hope for?"

Echo tapped the plaster cast. "Imagine how creative we can be once this is gone."

Kyla tilted her head back and offered a mischievous grin. "We should start planning that now. A vacation. Just us. What do you think?"

"I think it's long overdue."

Kyla kissed Echo's cheek and said, "We made it."

"Yes, we did." Echo knew exactly what she meant. There had been times over the past five years when she wasn't sure if they would, but she'd never given up. She'd always trusted that somehow, they would find their way back to the love that made life make sense. Without it, she would not know what to do. Loving Kyla, and being loved in return, completed her.

"Welcome back, baby," she whispered. "I'm so glad we're good again."

"We're better than good," Kyla said.

Echo kissed her slowly. "And we're just going to keep on getting better, baby."

About the Author

MJ Williamz was raised on California's Central Coast, which she still loves, but left at the age of seventeen in an attempt to further her education. She graduated from Chico State with a degree in business management. It was in Chico that MJ began to pursue her love of writing.

Now living in Portland, Oregon, MJ has made writing an integral part of her life. Since 2002, she's had over a dozen short stories accepted for publication, mostly erotica with a few romances thrown in for good measure.

Books Available From Bold Strokes Books

Dreams of Bali by C.J. Harte. Madison Barnes worships work, power, and success, and she's never allowed anyone to interfere—that is, until she runs into Karlie Henderson Stockard. Eclipse EBook (978-1-60282-070-8)

The Limits of Justice by John Morgan Wilson. Benjamin Justice and reporter Alexandra Templeton search for a killer in a mysterious compound in the remote California desert. (978-1-60282-060-9)

Designed for Love by Erin Dutton. Jillian Sealy and Wil Johnson don't much like each other, but they do have to work together—and what they desire most is not what either of them had planned. (978-1-60282-038-8)

Calling the Dead by Ali Vali. Six months after Hurricane Katrina, NOLA Detective Sept Savoie is a cop who thinks making a relationship work is harder than catching a serial killer—but her current case may prove her wrong. (978-1-60282-037-1)

Dark Garden by Jennifer Fulton. Vienna Blake and Mason Cavender are sworn enemies—who can't resist each other. Something has to give. (978-1-60282-036-4)

Shots Fired by MJ Williamz. Kyla and Echo seem to have the perfect relationship and the perfect life until someone shoots at Kyla—and Echo is the most likely suspect. (978-1-60282-035-7)

truelesbianlove.com by Carsen Taite. Mackenzie Lewis and Dr. Jordan Wagner have very different ideas about love, but they discover that truelesbianlove is closer than a click away. Eclipse EBook (978-1-60282-069-2)

Justice at Risk by John Morgan Wilson. Benjamin Justice's blind date leads to a rare opportunity for legitimate work, but a reckless risk changes his life forever. (978-1-60282-059-3)

Run to Me by Lisa Girolami. Burned by the four-letter word called love, the only thing Beth Standish wants to do is run for—or maybe from—her life. (978-1-60282-034-0)

Split the Aces by Jove Belle. In the neon glare of Sin City, two women ride a wave of passion that threatens to consume them in a world of fast money and fast times. (978-1-60282-033-3)

Uncharted Passage by Julie Cannon. Two women on a vacation that turns deadly face down one of nature's most ruthless killers—and find themselves falling in love. (978-1-60282-032-6)

Night Call by Radclyffe. All medevac helicopter pilot Jett McNally wants to do is fly and forget about the horror and heartbreak she left behind in the Middle East, but anesthesiologist Tristan Holmes has other plans. (978-1-60282-031-9)

Lake Effect Snow by C.P. Rowlands. News correspondent Annie T. Booker and FBI Agent Sarah Moore struggle to stay one step ahead of disaster as Annie's life becomes the war zone she once reported on. Eclipse EBook (978-1-60282-068-5)

Revision of Justice by John Morgan Wilson. Murder shifts into high gear, propelling Benjamin Justice into a raging fire that consumes the Hollywood Hills, burning steadily toward the famous Hollywood Sign—and the identity of a cold-blooded killer. (978-1-60282-058-6)

I Dare You by Larkin Rose. Stripper by night, corporate raider by day, Kelsey's only looking for sex and power, until she meets a woman who stirs her heart and her body. (978-1-60282-030-2)

Truth Behind the Mask by Lesley Davis. Erith Baylor is drawn to Sentinel Pagan Osborne's quiet strength, but the secrets between them strain duty and family ties. (978-1-60282-029-6)

Cooper's Deale by KI Thompson. Two would-be lovers and a decidedly inopportune murder spell trouble for Addy Cooper, no matter which way the cards fall. (978-1-60282-028-9)

Romantic Interludes 1: Discovery ed. by Radclyffe and Stacia Seaman. An anthology of sensual, erotic contemporary love stories from the best-selling Bold Strokes authors. (978-1-60282-027-2)

A Guarded Heart by Jennifer Fulton. The last place FBI Special Agent Pat Roussel expects to find herself is assigned to an illicit private security gig baby-sitting a celebrity. (Ebook) (978-1-60282-067-8)

Saving Grace by Jennifer Fulton. Champion swimmer Dawn Beaumont, injured in a car crash she caused, flees to Moon Island, where scientist Grace Ramsay welcomes her. (Ebook) (978-1-60282-066-1)

The Sacred Shore by Jennifer Fulton. Successful tech industry survivor Merris Randall does not believe in love at first sight until she meets Olivia Pearce. (Ebook) (978-1-60282-065-4)

Passion Bay by Jennifer Fulton. Two women from different ends of the earth meet in paradise. Author's expanded edition. (Ebook) (978-1-60282-064-7)

Never Wake by Gabrielle Goldsby. After a brutal attack, Emma Webster becomes a self-sentenced prisoner inside her condo—until the world outside her window goes silent. (Ebook) (978-1-60282-063-0)

The Caretaker's Daughter by Gabrielle Goldsby. Against the backdrop of a nineteenth-century English country estate, two women struggle to find love. (Ebook) (978-1-60282-062-3)

Simple Justice by John Morgan Wilson. When a pretty-boy cokehead is murdered, former LA reporter Benjamin Justice and his reluctant new partner, Alexandra Templeton, must unveil the real killer. (978-1-60282-057-9)

Remember Tomorrow by Gabrielle Goldsby. Cees Bannigan and Arieanna Simon find that a successful relationship rests in remembering the mistakes of the past. (978-1-60282-026-5)

Put Away Wet by Susan Smith. Jocelyn "Joey" Fellows has just been savagely dumped—when she posts an online personal ad, she discovers more than just the great sex she expected. (978-1-60282-025-8)